JASMINE: CASE ONE

A LT. KATE GAZZARA NOVEL

THE LT. KATE GAZZARA MURDER FILES
BOOK 1

BLAIR HOWARD

CHAPTER 1

IT WAS A DARK DAY FOR ME, THAT FRIDAY IN JULY 2008, and not just because it was raining. That was the day Harry Starke walked out of the police department for the last time. We'd been partners for almost eight years, but it was more than that. I was in love with the man, and he with me. Well, he was then. Now... not so much. We're still friends, but I guess I'd just gotten too used to having him around—and shoving him around, which he loves, though he'll never admit it.

He was always something of a loose cannon; he liked to do things his way, to be in control. But cops never are, not really. There's always a procedure to follow, a superior officer to please... or not which is why he left the PD—that and his constant bickering with the chief... but I'm rambling. This isn't about Harry, It's about my first case as lead detective.

We'd planned to spend the weekend together at Harry's condo on Lakeshore Lane, but I was on call and, sure enough, that Sunday evening my cell phone rang.

A couple years earlier, I'd made sergeant in the Major Crimes Unit, Homicide Division and I was partnered with Harry Starke. From then on, until the day he left, I played Dr. Watson to Harry's Sherlock Holmes. I was his backup, his sounding board, conscience, call it what you will. All of that left with him, and I was on my own.

We'd been to dinner at a fancy downtown restaurant and were out on the patio enjoying a glass of wine. Well, he was. I was on call, so I was drinking lemonade. We were watching the lights on the Thrasher Bridge and listening to something by Bach. The music seemed to suit his mood, and that of the quiet waters of the river.

It was a beautiful, relaxing evening... until my Phone buzzed at a little after ten o'clock.

"Damn!"

I didn't have to look at the screen. I knew what it was. Nobody ever calls me at that time on a Sunday evening. I sighed, looked at Harry, and took the call.

"Kate Gazzara,"

I listened, then said, "Okay. Give me the address. Okay. Got it. Thanks. I'll be there in twenty minutes."

Harry just leaned back in his chair, watching, smiling at me, his eyes half-closed.

"What's so damn funny?"

"Oh... I was just thinking of the good old days, when my phone used to ring at all hours of the day and night. But that's all over now, thank God. I'll see you... whenever?"

"D'you want me to come back tonight?"

He nodded, "You have a key. Whenever you get finished, just come on."

"Okay. Don't wait up."

He smiled mockingly. I rolled my eyes and left... Okay, maybe there was a little more swing in my step than usual. So, sue me.

WHEN I ARRIVED at the address on Bonny Oaks Drive in east Chattanooga there was little sign that anything was amiss. It was pitch dark, and I wondered if I was in the right place. Then I saw an iron gate set back maybe thirty feet from the road. It was wide open, manned by a uniformed officer I knew well. He logged me in and then waved me through, up the short drive to the old sand quarry. There, it was a different story.

The quarry and its surrounds, a one-time TDOT storage facility, had been abandoned for years, but it was lit up like noontime by four portable light towers.

Wow, I remember thinking, *somebody's on the ball.*

That somebody was Mike Willis, our CSI supervisor. He was standing beside Doc Sheddon's beat-up old Suburban. Doc was, and still is, Hamilton County's chief medical examiner and he, too, was obviously on the ball, though there was little to be seen of him. He was teetering on top of a small step ladder, which was propped against a large section of concrete culvert set on end, its mouth open to the sky. All I could see of Doc was his white Tyvek-covered backside.

Doc's not a big man, but he is a little overweight. The sight of him hanging over the rim of that pipe would, on any other day, have made me smile. That day? No!

He stood on tiptoe and leaned even further into the

pipe. The ladder shook and I grabbed it, steadied it, and held on. He came down a moment or two later, puffing and blowing like an old steam engine.

"Hey, Kate," he said, as he stepped off the bottom rung. "Where's Harry?"

Oh boy. Please tell me this is not how it's going to be from now on.

"It's a long story," I said, dodging the question. "This one's all mine. What do we have?"

I thought for a second he was going to press me about Harry, but he didn't.

"It's a nasty one, Kate. Go on up and take a look while I catch my breath."

I didn't need to look to know what was in there; I could smell it. But I suited up, asked one of the uniformed officers to hold the ladder, and I climbed on up to the rim of the pipe and peered inside. Someone had set a mobile light tower close by, high enough so that it shined down into the pipe.

At first, I couldn't tell what I was looking at. Then, as my eyes adjusted to the shadows, I could see her. She appeared to be fully dressed: dark blue shorts and what once had been a white crop top. She lay on the dirt at the bottom of the pipe, curled up in the fetal position, her body curving around the inside of the pipe. I couldn't see her face: it was covered by her hair, which appeared to be moving, undulating. *Maggots*, I thought.

The stench inside the pipe was overpowering. From what I could see of her arms and legs, I figured she must have been inside that pipe for several days, maybe more.

I descended the ladder and turned to the officer who was holding it for me and said, "Hey, Tom. Who was first on the scene?"

"That would be me," he replied. "Marty arrived a couple of minutes after me. The gate was chained. We had to use bolt cutters."

I nodded, "Who called it in?"

"A kid. He wouldn't give his name. There's a bunch of 'em that use this place to ride mountain bikes. They noticed the smell and, being kids, they decided to investigate. They must have boosted one kid up to see down inside the pipe. That's his puke there," he pointed.

"Probably puked on the booster too," I said.

Tom shrugged. "One of them made the call at eight-oh-seven. All he said was," he checked his notepad. "'There's a pipe with a dead body in it.' Hege the dispatcher the address then hung up. By the time I got here they were long gone. I figured it had to be one of these sections of culvert. There are twenty-eight of them scattered all over the site, all different sizes, some lying flat, some standing up like this one. The only other pipes on the property are those two stacks of black, plastic drainage pipe over there," he pointed to them. "They're obviously too small. It wasn't difficult to find her, though. The smell led us right to this one."

Together, we stood and stared at it. Someone had marked the dimensions on the side: forty-eight-inch diameter, six feet tall.

"Better get the site properly secured," I said. Then I had a thought, "How do they get onto the property? The kids?"

"The property's fenced," he replied. "The gate is the

only point of access for vehicles, but the quarry is surrounded by houses with yards that back right up to it. You know how kids are, Sergeant. If there's a way in, they'll find it. If there's not, they'll make one, right?"

I nodded, "I need to talk to Doc Sheddon. I'll check with you before I leave."

I spotted Doc by his car, pulling off his coveralls. "Don't even ask, Kate," he said as I approached. "I couldn't see a damn thing with her at the bottom of that pipe. She's been there a while, though. Six or seven days, and in this heat? Whew! Hey, Mike."

Mike Willis joined us. He too was wearing white coveralls.

"You find anything, Mike?" I asked.

He looked at me as if I'd just spit in his hand. "What do *you* think? I've been here maybe thirty minutes and it's almost midnight, for God's sake. I can't do anything until daylight. I suggest you secure the scene, Sergeant, and I'll get to it first thing tomorrow. You'll be removing the body, right?" he said to Doc.

"Of course." Doc looked at his watch. "The EMTs should be here any minute. We'll do the postmortem tomorrow at eleven. You up for it, Kate?"

"Of course," I replied.

Mike was right. There was nothing to be done until the site had been processed, so I wrapped it up for the evening. I told Doc I'd see him in the morning, and then I too left the site.

I USED my key to let myself into Harry's condo and looked at the kitchen clock. It was just after one in the morning. I shuddered, thinking about the day yet to come, then I took a shower to wash the stink from my body.

I slipped into my pajamas and climbed in next to him

"So," he said, rolling over, "How bad was it?"

I took a deep breath, let it out slowly, and said, "It was pretty bad."

I spent the next five minutes telling him about it, but he was asleep before I finished. I set the alarm on my phone for six o'clock.

I needn't have bothered: Harry was up and out for his morning run by five-thirty. When he finally climbed out of the shower an hour later, I had coffee and bagels ready.

"Harry," I said, watching him over the rim of my second cup of coffee. "What are your plans? What are you going to do now that you're no longer a cop? You can't just sit around and mope. You need to do something."

He tilted his head slightly, smiled that annoying little smirk he affects when he thinks he knows something nobody else knows, and reached for his wallet.

This time he really did know something I didn't know. He flipped a business card onto the table. It read "Harry Starke Investigations" along with an address on Georgia Avenue and several phone numbers.

"No!" I all but shouted the word. "You, a private investigator?" And I burst out laughing. Harry, that enigmatic little smile still on his lips, just sat there, looking at me.

I stopped laughing. I looked at him seriously, "You're not kidding, are you?"

"Nope."

"How long.... You've been.... Harry, you must've been planning this for a while. Why the hell didn't you tell me?"

He shrugged, "I wasn't sure about it. As you say, I need to do something. This seems like it might work. The money won't be great, but I don't need a paycheck."

Harry's father, August Starke, was one of the wealthiest attorneys in the country. Harry was, even in those days, very well off in his own right. So, no, he didn't need a paycheck.

"Look, Kate. I loved being a cop. I loved being an investigator. What I didn't love was the politics, the back-stabbing... and the damn chief. It makes sense, the PI thing. I'll be my own boss, hire my own people, find my own clients —which, by the way, I've already done. I have at least a couple dozen high-powered attorneys waiting in line, not to mention dear old dad. Now all I need is staff."

He was silent for a moment, watching me.

He has the most intense blue eyes....

And then I realized:

You want me to work for you. Oh no. I love you, Harry, but no way in hell.

"It's not going to happen, Harry."

"Why not? We get along, we work well together, we always have. We make a great team."

I looked at my watch. It was almost eight: time I wasn't there. Fortunately, I didn't have to go home. I kept a change of clothes at Harry's condo—well, more than one, actually —so all I had to do was drive to the PD on Amnicola Highway and check in.

"Let's talk about it later, okay?" I said as I walked to the door.

He shrugged. Nothing ever seemed to bother him. I always hated that.

I kissed him, pinched his cheek, and said I'd call him later. Then I left him staring into the depths of his cup.

CHAPTER 2

Later that Monday morning, I was at my desk in the incident room, sipping on my third cup of what's laughingly called coffee, when Chief Johnston leaned over my shoulder and handed me a slim manila folder.

"Here you go, Kate."

"What is it?" I asked, although I was pretty sure I knew. I flipped through the file. Just a dozen or so sheets of paper —forms, statements—and a couple photos of a pretty young girl who matched the stats of the body in the culvert.

"It's the missing persons file for a Jasmine Thomas. I'm thinking she's the homicide you caught last night. If not, pass it along. But if it is, you've got a jump start." He plucked a photo out of the file. "I just had a call from the mayor about this girl, Jasmine. She was reported missing two weeks ago and the case is getting a lot of media attention. I need it wrapped up ASAP. That a problem?"

Johnston never changes. He looks much the same now as he did that day twelve years ago when I joined the force:

big round head, shaved and polished to a shine; half-glasses; a pure-white Hulk Hogan mustache; and a chest like a barrel. He was also something of a martinet, a stickler for routine, a force to be obeyed instantly and without question. He was glad to see Harry gone, of that, I was sure.

"You'll need a new partner," he said. "I'm thinking Detective Tracy.... Now, don't give me that look, Sergeant. He'll do just fine. I've also assigned Detective Foote to you, temporarily. If you need uniform officers, Captain Peck is your go-to. I've already let him know."

Dick Tracy? Oh my God! What did I do to deserve this?

No, his name wasn't really Dick. He'd been stuck with the nickname, partly because of the Chester Gould comic strip detective from the 1930s, but mostly because that's exactly what John Tracy was: a dick. I hadn't hoped for much in my new partner, but this....

"Yes, sir. But, Detective Tracy—"

"Good. Get it wrapped up, quickly, Catherine." He flipped the photo of Jasmine Thomas onto my desk and left me staring after him, my mind in whirl.

Dick Tracy. I shook my head. *This is not happening!*

Oh, but apparently it was. I heard the man himself call from behind me.

"Hey, Katie!" Tracy swaggered around my chair, parked his ass on the corner of my desk, one foot on the floor, the other swinging back and forth, crotch on full display "Looks like it's you and the *Dick*, huh?"

The way he emphasized the word, the grin, and the look he gave me were sleazy beyond words. His right leg began to brush my thigh as it swung. I shuddered. And I knew right then I was going to have to shut him down, and quickly.

I leaned back in my chair, pushed with my feet to roll away from the desk, and stared up at him.

John Tracy was everything I disliked in a man: arrogant, lazy, indolent, sloppy, and the quintessential smartass. He was thirty-four, three years older than me, but he looked forty. He was also shorter than me by a good three inches; he wore lifts to boost his five-nine inches. He was skinny, deeply tanned, and his shoulder-length brown hair was in need of a wash. He was wearing worn out jeans and a gray t-shirt—also in need of a wash—and Nike sneakers that had seen better days.

He'd spent the last seven years in Narcotics which, I hoped, accounted for his appearance, if not his attitude.

I looked around the incident room—my desk was in a small cubicle at the far end, under the window. Everyone in the room was watching; they turned quickly away, but not in time to hide the smiles.

I tilted my head a little, crossed my legs, and looked up at him through half-closed eyes. "Hello, Detective Tracy. Yes, Chief Johnston did mention it. And I want to tell you..."

Then, in one quick movement I rolled forward, grabbed his left ear, and twisted it. hard. "Don't *ever* call me 'Katie' again. You hear?"

"Ahhh, oh, ahhh!" Tracy slid a little way off the desk and scrabbled at my hands. I twisted. He squeeled, slid off my desk and had to grab at it to stop himself from falling.

"I repeat. Never again. Do you understand?"

"Ye-ah," he howled, "I got it. I got it!"

"Good."

Again, I glanced around the room. They didn't even

bother to look away this time. Some of the smiles had turned into laughter.

I turned back to him, released his ear and said, "Now, Detective, here's how it's going to be. First: from now on, you will call me Sergeant. Is that clear?"

He nodded frantically.

"Good. Second: go home and take a shower. You stink like a sewer rat. Put on some respectable clothing and get your hair cut. How you made it in here is a mystery, but this is Homicide, not Narcotics, and you will dress and act professionally. Is *that* clear?"

Again, he nodded.

"Good. You have..." I looked at my watch, "until eleven. That's two hours. I'll expect to see you at the forensic center, where we will attend a postmortem. Now get out of here, and don't be late."

He nodded, holding onto his ear, then turned and almost ran to the elevators..

There was a ripple of applause from the rest of the detectives and uniformed officers, and even a couple of appreciative whistles. I smiled, opened the file, and made a big show of ignoring them. Out of habit, I glanced toward Harry's now-vacant desk. *Damn. I'm sure going to miss having him around.*

The photographs in the file were of a young girl with long brown hair and a big smile. One was obviously a 'Sweet Sixteen' photo. I stared at it for a moment, then set it aside. The other was a full body shot taken outdoors. She was laughing; she'd been a pretty, young thing. I shook my head and began to read.

Seventeen-year-old Jasmine Thomas had been

reported missing on Saturday morning, July 12. According to Arlis Thomas, the girl's mother, Jasmine had returned home from her part-time job at Juno's restaurant Friday afternoon at around five. She'd eaten dinner, spent some time in her room texting friends, and then decided to go out.

She'd left home at just after seven in her own car, a pale-blue Honda Civic, intending to meet her friends at Hamilton Place Mall. She never arrived. When she didn't come home that night, her mother called her several times, but she didn't pick up. She then called Jasmine's friends, thinking she might have stayed overnight. When she learned that no one had seen her, she called the police.

As usual, the officer who took the call figured the girl had either run away or was having a good time somewhere, maybe with a boyfriend, and would return home sooner or later. It was the typical response, especially considering the girl's age and the fact that she owned her own car.

But Arlis Thomas hadn't given up. She'd called Missing Persons every day, telling them that she'd heard nothing from her daughter. Calls to Jasmine's cell now went straight to voice mail, which meant the battery was dead or the phone was damaged. The phone's last known location was gleaned from a cell tower at Highway 153 and Shallowford Road, a little more than a mile north of Hamilton Place Mall. That was at seven-twenty-two on Friday evening, July 11, the night she went missing.

Did she make it to the mall? Where would she have parked? We had searched all the mall parking lots and come up empty. From her home on Wickman Lane, Jasmine would have taken Bonny Oaks Drive to the mall. Was she stopped as she passed the quarry? The 2005 Honda Civic hadn't been found there either.

I picked up the phone and called Charlie Peck.

"Hey, Captain. This is Kate Gazzara, Homicide. Chief Johnston said he'd apprised you... Okay, good. Well, look, I need some help. I'm missing a 2005 Honda Civic, pale-blue. Could you have your people keep an eye open for it, let me know if it turns up abandoned? We know it's not at the mall, but could you check the lots at the other malls, maybe the long-term lot at the airport? Thanks, Charlie. I'm also going to need some help with a door-to-door. Can you spare a couple of officers for the rest of the day? Good. Have them report to Detective Foote." I read him the Honda's license plate number, thanked him again, and hung up.

Lovell Field isn't a big airport. It's a typically busy regional facility with plenty of parking, and the lots are always well populated. Still, I figured an abandoned car could go unnoticed in the long-term section, maybe for weeks. The malls? Not so much: they have security patrols. But you never know. The river was a consideration, too, but there must be a hundred and one out-of-the-way spots where a car could be dumped in the water. If it was there, finding it would be almost impossible.

I looked at my watch; it was after ten. I turned my attention to the kids who found the body. Who were they, and how had they gotten on the property?

Detective Sarah Foote and I had been friends for a couple of years. She was twenty-six when we met, three years younger than me, and we got along well. She was seated at her desk on the far side of the room. I picked up the phone, buzzed her, and waved her over.

"The chief filled you in?" I asked.

"Oh, yeah. Good job on Tracy, by the way."

I didn't comment, though I might have winked, a little. "Sarah, I need you to conduct a door-to-door of the houses backing onto the quarry on Bonny Oaks. That would be the 3800 and 3900 blocks on Bonny Oaks itself, and then Young Road, Parkway Drive, Ridgecrest, and Meade Circle. Charlie Peck is sending some uniforms over to help. I'd like it done by the end of the day, if possible. You're looking for two things: the kids who found the body—apparently there are a bunch who use the quarry as a playground—and any access routes into the quarry. That means footpaths, bike trails, whatever. Got it?"

"I'm on it."

"Great. I have to get on over to Doc's. He's doing the post this morning; I'll call you later. Oh, and here's the file. Take a look at it before you go."

"Pretty girl," she said. Flipping through the pages.

"Yes. She was."

TRACY WAS SITTING in the lobby at the forensic center waiting for me. He stood when I entered. I looked him up and down. He'd changed into a fresh pair of jeans and a pink golf shirt, and he'd combed his hair. At least he looked clean.

"Jeans?" I asked. "Don't you have any decent pants?"

"Not really." He looked defiantly at me. "I never needed them in Narcotics. I'll shop when I get a chance, okay?"

I nodded. "Be sure you do. No haircut?"

"I did have it cut! Well, trimmed."

I shook my head, exasperated. "Just keep it tidy."

"Hey, Kate," Doc said, appearing as if from nowhere. "Right on time, as always. Who's your friend?"

I made the introductions; they shook hands. Doc squinted at Tracy over his half-glasses. I wondered what he was thinking.

"Suit up then," Doc said, "and let's get to it." He sized Tracy up and smiled thinly. "There's some VapoRub in the cupboard over there. You're going to need it. She's quite ripe, I'm afraid."

I looked at Tracy. His face was white.

"This is your first?" I asked.

He nodded, "I wasn't expected to attend overdoses, and we handed homicides over to you guys, so…"

"You can stay out here in the lobby, if you like," I said. "But this is what we do; you might as well get used to it."

The word "ripe" didn't come near to describing what we saw.

"Carol has already prepped and x-rayed the body," Doc said, his voice muffled by the mask that covered his mouth and nose beneath his face shield.

"Hi, Carol," I said.

"Kate," she replied.

Carol Oats was, and still is, Doc Sheddon's forensic anthropologist.

"She was able to get a full set of prints," Doc continued,

"which should be helpful. And the teeth are intact; also helpful. So, let's get started."

He picked through the instruments on the stainless-steel tray at his elbow and selected a scalpel. Then he leaned forward over the body and with one swift, precise stroke he made a deep, diagonal incision from the left shoulder to the base of the sternum. As he did so, Tracy staggered back several steps, then turned and stumbled for the door.

"First door on the right," Doc called over his shoulder as the putrefied flesh split and peeled away under his scalpel.

I've lost count of the number of posts I've witnessed during my years at the PD. It never gets any easier, but that one? Well, it was memorable. The body was bloated, the skin blistered and peeling away from greenish-black flesh. The smell, something I thought I'd gotten used to, was overpowering. I took two steps back, closed my eyes, and waited for my churning stomach to settle.

"You all right, Kate?" Doc asked as he set the shears to cut the first rib.

I nodded and stepped back to the edge of the table. The rib cracked as the shears bit, and Tracy, who had just walked back in, turned and rushed out again. And I really didn't blame him.

Doc Sheddon systematically dissected what was left of the girl, and I watched him do it; Tracy came and went as his stomach allowed.

Okay; I guess he gets one point for grit.

Finally, the good doctor laid down his tools, took a step back, and signaled for Carol to take over. He removed his face shield and mask and began his summary.

"Caucasian, young, aged between fifteen and twenty.

She died, probably mid-morning, eight to ten days ago; closer to ten than eight, I'd say. The heat in the pipe during the day must have risen close to a hundred and twenty. She's been slow cooked, close to rare." He grinned across the table at me. I shook my head at him, but he took no notice. Back then, Doc was famous for his gallows humor. Today, not so much.

"Cause?" I prompted.

"Strangulation. The hyoid is fractured and the larynx is crushed. Whoever did this has large hands, strong. She was restrained, see here?" He pointed to ligature marks on her wrists, thighs, and ankles.

"Was she—"

"Raped?" He shrugged. "Hard to say. Carol took samples, but I wouldn't hold my breath. The girl lost a lot of fluid, and the corpse is heavily infested, as you can see."

Yes, I could see.

"There's no semen, as far as we can tell," he continued. "We'll check for foreign DNA, but I doubt we'll find anything. There's nothing under her fingernails and, as I said, she's lost a lot of fluid. There is some fine dust on her back, buttocks, calves, the soles of her feet, her elbows, and even in her hair; she must have been laid down on a dry, dusty surface somewhere. I can't be sure without a full analysis, but I'd guess a dirt floor rather than floor boards. Maybe Mike Willis will be able to tell us. She was dressed in shorts and a—" he gestured vaguely at his ribcage, "a crop top, is that what they call them? Her clothing is over there if you want to look—but no bra or panties, or shoes, which makes me wonder..."

I nodded. "Maybe whoever did this dressed her again after he killed her?"

He shrugged. "It's a thought. There's no way to tell, but the absence of bra and panties..." He looked at me. "Would she go out without them, d'you suppose?"

I shook my head, "I wouldn't, but then I'm not seventeen. Who knows what these kids do? If we identify her as Jasmine Thomas, I'll ask her mother. She'd know."

"Yes, well. As soon as we're done here, I'll send her clothes to Mike Willis. Her prints should work for you. Carol has emailed the x-rays and photos of her teeth to the local dental association, so maybe you'll know something later today. DNA, hers, is something of a catch twenty-two. We can't use it to identify her until we know who she is, unless she has a record. Which, judging by her age, I doubt she'll have. Unless she was a hooker, of course."

"You say she's been dead for approximately ten days. That would make it the morning of July 17, give or take twenty-four hours. Can we do any better than that?" I looked at him.

He nodded, "Eight to ten days, I think I said. That would make the seventeenth the baseline date... and no. I can't do better than that. The wide-ranging temperatures inside the pipe had a devastating effect on her body. Two days is as close as I can comfortably go."

"Okaaay," I said, doubtfully, "but you said she died mid-morning. If you can't fix the day, how can you fix the time?"

"That, my dear, was the easy part. I found the remains of a sausage biscuit in her stomach, probably from Hardee's. They stop serving breakfast at ten-thirty. Digestion had barely begun, so mid-morning is a reasonable assumption. Then again, the biscuit could have been bought in the morning and saved for later…"

I made a face.

He chuckled. "No, they don't keep very well, do they. Even so, it's no more than an educated guess. If you can justify the cost, I could have Dr. Wu come down from UT Knoxville. He might be able to narrow it down further, perhaps to within six or eight hours either way, but he's expensive."

Dr. Jason Wu is a forensic entomologist at the University of Tennessee, Knoxville. He spends most of his days studying the dead at the Body Farm.

"The closer we can get to the actual time of death the better, especially when we may be dealing with alibis. Forty-eight hours is a huge window. This kid was murdered. We have to spend the money."

"Of course. I'll call him as soon as we're done here."

"So," I said. "Ten days. If she is my missing girl, she was alive for at least four days before she was killed, maybe even five. Where the hell was she?"

"Well, I can tell you this much. The bladder was empty; she must have voided it during asphyxiation, which is common. Find the crime scene and you'll probably find the urine."

I leaned over the table to look at the girl's face, the skin dark, blistered, and weeping. I shook my head.

"Geez, Doc. I need a photo to show the missing kid's parents."

He shook his head. "I wouldn't do it. Not yet. I'll have Carol work on her face, see if she can make her look a little better, but it's going to take a skilled mortician to make her look anything like presentable. I'll have Lilo Ridge come by when I've finished with her. That old boy can work wonders with a little makeup."

Lilo Ridge? Sounds like a Civil War battlefield...

"What about birthmarks?" I asked. "Old bone breaks, scars, missing teeth?"

"She has a c-shaped scar on her left knee, here," he pointed to it. "Surgical. Meniscectomy scar. Not the result of a fall. There's nothing else."

I sighed. Her knee was in no better condition than her face, but I had to have something to work with. I snapped a couple of images of the scar with my phone, then a close-up of her face.

"I won't use that one unless I have to. The scar isn't much, but it will have to do. If I can get a positive ID on the scar, I'll get DNA samples from her home. It's worth a try."

"Well, my dear, good luck to you. Now, if we're done, I have a young man waiting for me... not that he cares if I'm late. He has a bullet in the back of his head."

I found Dick Tracy sitting in the lobby, elbows on his knees, face in his hands, looking decidedly worse for his experience.

"Let's go, Detective," I said. "Places to go, people to see."

CHAPTER 3

As I walked to my unmarked cruiser in the lot behind the forensic center, I looked at my watch. It was just after twelve-thirty. The post had taken slightly more than an hour-and-a-half. Not bad, considering the state of the body.

I told Tracy to take his car to the PD parking lot and I'd pick him up. I followed him as he pulled into the back lot, and watched as he locked his car. He climbed into my unmarked cruiser and slammed the door. I looked at him.

He still looks like a damn hobo.

"The outfit, Detective," I said as he closed the car door. "The shirt... is okay, but it needs ironing. The jeans, well, I have no objection to jeans, but they should be clean and pressed. No need for a crease, but the hole in the knee is not going to get it. Do I need to take you shopping?"

"No. Look, Sergeant. For the last seven years I've had to blend in with the lowlifes I was dealing with. I do have a suit and tie, and my uniform, a couple more golf shirts.

Other than that, what you see is what you get. I'll do some shopping this evening. That good enough for you?"

I looked sideways at him as I pulled out of the lot and onto Amnicola. He was still quite pale.

"Are you married, Tracy? Got a girlfriend? Your mother?"

"I know how to dress myself, dammit!" He stopped, took a deep breath, then turned to face me, a resigned look on his face. "I'm sorry. I didn't mean to... Look, Sergeant, I'm grateful for the chance. I've always wanted Homicide. But you have to give me a little time to adjust. I won't let you down."

I nodded, recognizing the change of tone, but I wasn't ready to soften up just yet. "See that you don't."

I put him out of my mind and concentrated on the case, what little there was of it. From reading the case file, I knew there'd been a tri-state search for Jasmine that had turned up nothing: no sightings of her or her car.

The Greenway Farms Park—a 180-acre city park along North Chickamauga Creek—had been searched from one end to the other: nothing. Same for the Greenway south of Bonny Oaks. The dead ends were piling up.

Jasmine Thomas had lived with her parents in an older one-and-a-half story home not more than a quarter-mile from where the body had been found. The house was some one hundred yards north of Bonny Oaks, opposite another home; both houses were set back from the Lane some fifty feet and fronted by neatly-trimmed lawns... well, they were more weeds than grass, but still neatly trimmed. The lane was narrow, with room enough for only one vehicle at a time.

I turned onto the lane and drove past the two houses, all the way to a dead end some three hundred yards on, at the front gate of a large, two-story home that faced south back along Wickman.

I made a turn and drove back to the Thomas residence, pulled into the driveway, and shut off the motor. I sat for a moment, thinking, composing myself. This was a first for me. In the past, this had been Harry's job. Now, it was mine. All mine.

I turned to Tracy, who still looked green. "Are you coming with me, or d'you want to stay here?"

He didn't answer. He grabbed the door handle, put his shoulder to the door, pushed it open, and stepped out onto the gravel driveway. I did the same.

I waited as he circled the car to join me, then said, "Let me do the talking, okay?"

He nodded.

I pushed the doorbell, listened to the chimes, and we waited. I was about to push it again when the door opened, just a crack.

"Yeah?" a man's voice asked. "What d'ya want?"

"I'm Sergeant Gazzara, Chattanooga PD. This is Detective Tracy. I need to talk with Mr. Cletus Thomas, please."

"This about Jasmine?" he asked, as he opened the door fully.

He was a small man, skinny, with a bald head, bushy eyebrows, beady eyes, and glasses with large circular lenses. He was wearing jeans and a black t-shirt, and looked to be about fifty years old, but I could have been wrong by ten years either way.

"May we come in for a minute, sir?"

He stepped aside and we walked into another world. These folks were "country." The interior of the home was clean but cluttered. The bric-a-brac of maybe three generations filled every nook and cranny.

Hoarders? It sure looks like it.

"You wanna si'down?" he asked.

I looked around.

You're joking, right?

"Uh..."

"Here," he said, grabbing a pile of magazines from the seat of a dining chair. "Sit here. You can sit there," he said to Tracy, pointing at another chair. "Shove the cat off. She won't hurt you."

I sat down on the edge of the chair and looked up at him, "Is Mrs. Thomas home?"

He hesitated, "Ye-es, but she's in the back yard pickin' tomatoes... What is it you want?"

"I'd like to talk to you both, if you don't mind."

He shook his head, muttering under his breath, and went out into what I assumed was the kitchen.

"Hey, Arlis!" he yelled. "They's two police officers here an' they wanna talk about Jasmine! C'mon in!"

Arlis Thomas was not at all what I expected. She was lovely: tall and slender, she looked half her husband's age.

"You've found her?" She was smiling as she sat down on the arm of the sofa next to her husband. "Oh, thank God. Is she okay? Where is she?"

And here we go.

I looked at Tracy. He looked away.

"She is okay... isn't she?" Her face had turned pale despite the deep suntan.

"I don't know." I paused, then said, "Mrs. Thomas, Mr. Thomas. There's no easy way to do this. We've found the body of a young girl—"

"The one they's talkin' about on TV?" he interrupted me, grabbing his wife's hand.

She was slowly shaking her head, the tears already rolling down her face.

"Yes, but we don't know who she is, which is why—"

"It's her," he interrupted again.

"No-ooo," she wailed. "It's not her; it's not; it can't be."

Oh shit. Harry, where the hell are you when I need you? No! Stop it. You can do this.

"It may not be her," I said, knowing deep down that it was. Hell, the girl in the photos was the image of Arlis Thomas. "But we need your help to find out. Does Jasmine have any identifying marks, moles, birthmarks, scars?"

She shook her head, "No. None."

"Yeah, she does," Thomas said. "She has that scar on her knee from when she had that mini, mini... when she had that cartilage removed."

And right then my heart sank. It was her. I almost got up and told them goodbye, but I had to make sure.

"On her knee?" I asked. "Which one."

"The left. It was her left knee."

I sighed inwardly. I brought the photo of the scar up on phone and held it out for him to look at.

"Yeah, that looks like it, but that's not her. This is a black woman. Our Jasmine is white, like us."

What the hell do I say to that? "Oh, that's just the advanced putrefaction?"

"This woman is white, Mr. Thomas. It's... it's a bad picture, hard to tell."

I put the phone back in its clip and turned to Tracy. "Go get the kit from the trunk, Detective."

"What?" Mrs. Thomas asked. "What kit? Cletus told you it isn't her."

"Yes, he did, but I need to make sure. Would you mind if we took a look at her room?"

She looked desperately at her husband, "But it isn't her..." she whispered.

"I know," I said, "but it's best to make sure. Which way...?"

"I'll show you. You wait here, Arlis." Thomas rose wearily to his feet. I could tell: he knew.

As we left the room, I said, "I'm also going to need prints from everyone living here. Is it just you, Mrs. Thomas, and Jasmine?"

"No. We have two more kids, her older brother Michael and her sister Sophia. My brother Joe, he also lives with us."

I made note of the names on my iPad. "Your brother," I asked, "is he here?"

"No. He's at work. The kids aren't here, either."

"Where does your brother work? I'd like to talk to him, and get his prints for comparison, to make sure we know one from the other."

"He works at Henry's Tire Shop on Rossville Boulevard."

"And your other two children; tell me about them, please."

He looked guardedly at me, "Why?"

"For the same reason. I need to know how they interact

with Jasmine, ask if they noticed anything different about her, any changes in her demeanor or routine. And we need their prints so we can eliminate them from fingerprint evidence."

"Michael is nineteen. He's a student at Chattanooga Community College and works a part-time job at KFC in Hixson. Sophia's fifteen. She's at the neighbor's pool across the street with Jennifer, their kid. She just about lives over there during summer break."

I nodded, "So let's take a look at Jasmine's room, then I'll get your prints, and Mrs. Thomas's."

Tracy returned with the kit and we followed him up the stairs to the girl's room. The door was already open. I stood for a moment looking into the room, trying to get a feel for the girl who had once occupied it. It was clean, tidy, with blue curtains hanging over the window and a matching blue cover on the bed.

I'd bet money that Arlis made them both herself.

I stepped inside; Tracy followed and stepped around me, "Thank you, Mr. Thomas," I said as I closed the door. "I'll call if I need you."

He nodded and turned away. I took the small, black plastic case from Tracy, laid it carefully down on the bed, so as not to disturb anything. I opened it and took out two pairs of latex gloves, one of which I handed to Tracy.

"So," I said, as I began to walk the room and then the adjoining bathroom. "What do you think?"

"About what?"

I stopped, turned, and stared at him.

Is he just plain dumb, or just acting like he is?

"The Thomases, the girl, what do you think?"

He shrugged, "I think it's her."

I shook my head.

No shit, Sherlock!

"Okay," I said. "Let's see what we can find. Don't touch anything; not yet." And I turned back to the bathroom.

The kid was a neat freak, unless her mother had been tidying after her. The usual collection of makeup, hair spray, lotions, and so on was arranged on a small shelf. Several different brands of shampoo and conditioner stood in the shower, none of it expensive. A set of combs and brushes was laid out neatly on the vanity.

I went back into the bedroom and grabbed my finger-print kit out of the black case on the bed. It was a little something I'd put together myself: some magnetic powder; a magnetic wand; a roll of wide, clear sticky tape; some white backing cards; a dozen or so ten-cards; and an ink pad.

I returned to the bathroom, set the fingerprint kit down on the vanity, and opened it. Then I opened the cupboards under the vanity. I knew just what I was looking for, and there they were: two glass jars. One filled with Q-tips, the other with cotton balls.

I placed both jars on the vanity and carefully dusted them with black magnetic powder.

Oh yeah... that's what I'm talking about!

Both jars were liberally covered with latent prints, and I was willing to bet all of them belonged to Jasmine. I lifted the prints using the sticky tape and transferred them to backing cards. If we could find a match for just one of the prints Carol Oats lifted from the girl in the pipe, we'd know it was Jasmine. Just to be sure, though, I decided to look for a DNA sample. I found some hair on the hairbrush and a length of dental floss stuck to the bottom of the empty trash can, and that was all. Someone had cleaned the bathroom.

I sealed my samples in paper evidence envelopes, signed and dated them, then stowed them in the case along with my fingerprint kit.

The bedroom had also been tidied and cleaned; there wasn't much to be seen of the girl's character. The drawers in the dresser were filled with the usual mélange of women's clothing, as was the closet: nothing out of the ordinary there. The nightstand—there was only one—at the left side of the bed had a small drawer with a cupboard below.

The cupboard was filled with books, all young-adult fiction. She was a reader.

Unusual. Kids don't read much these days.

The drawer... well, it was almost empty.

And that's even more unusual. Where the hell is her stuff? There must be some. She's seventeen for God's sake; there should be personal stuff all over the place.

I was looking for a journal, an address book, even a notebook would have been something but... nothing. Only basic supplies in the desk, no photos of friends on the walls, no clutter of everyday life. The room could have belonged to anyone; it felt like it belonged to no one. I had the distinct feeling someone had cleaned out her room. Often, worried parents will do that, not wanting their kid to look bad to investigators.

Hmmm. I need to talk to the parents.

Tracy was leaning on the door frame, his arms folded, feet crossed at the ankles, watching me.

"Anything to contribute, Detective?"

He shook his head, smiling, "Nope!"

Damn. Am I going to have to pull every little thought out of him?

"So what are you thinking?"

"About what?"

"Are you serious?"

This is not *going to work.*

He shrugged; the smile stuck fast on his face.

I shook my head, exasperated, "Let's go talk to the parents." I retrieved the black case from the bed and pushed past him.

They were waiting for us in the living room.

I sat down in front of them. Tracy did his door frame thing again.

"It's her," Thomas said. "The girl in the pipe, it's Jasmine."

"We don't know that," I said. "I—"

"I know it. It's her. She's dead, an' I know who done it." He glared at me.

You do?

"We don't know that it's your daughter, Mr. Thomas. Maybe it is. We'll know soon enough. I have some very good fingerprints. Now I need yours so we can eliminate them. If there's a match with the dead girl, I'll know before the end of the day. This will only take a minute."

I laid my kit on the table, opened it, and stood aside. "Detective Tracy?"

"What?"

"The prints. Would you do them for me, please?"

I watched him as he reluctantly stepped forward and went to work.

Not much of a self-starter.

I asked Mrs. Thomas, "Can we get hold of Sophia? Ask her to come home?"

She nodded and went to the phone.

"While we're waiting, Mr. Thomas, you said you know who killed her... if it is her. Who, and how do you know?"

"Piece o' shit lives at the end of the road. Russell Hawkins. He's been stalkin' her for more'n a year: calls all the time, sits in his car watchin' her, waits for her at school, follows her around. It's him, I'm tellin' ya."

"Russell Hawkins?" I made a note of the name on my iPad.

He nodded. "Yeah. I warned him off a hundred times, but I can't be everywhere."

I asked him for Jasmine's phone number, made a note of it, and then I turned to Tracy, "We need to get her phone records."

He nodded.

I looked at Arlis Thomas, "Do you know anyone who would want to hurt Jasmine?"

She was seated on the sofa next to her husband with her arms folded. She shook her head. "It's not her. She's with friends, or someone from work."

"What about this Russell Hawkins?"

"Oh... I don't know," she said. "He asked her out, several times, but..."

"He was stalkin' her, dammit!" Thomas glared angrily at his wife. She shrugged, but didn't answer.

"That's a serious allegation, Mr. Thomas."

"Yeah, I know, but it's true. It's been goin' on for years. Every day, last year or so. Obsessed with her, is what he is. It's him."

"Who is?"

I turned to the door and saw a girl in a bikini, a towel wrapped around her shoulders. Sophia was pretty. No, she was beautiful, and she looked a lot older than her fifteen years.

"Never you mind," Arlis said. "These here are police officers. They want to talk to you."

"What about? Is this about Jasmine? Have you found her? Where is she?"

"No, we haven't found her," I said, "but we need..." and I did my best to explain the situation without upsetting her. It didn't go too well, especially when I asked her to provide fingerprints.

"What do you want them for?" she asked, finally holding out her right hand for Tracy to print her.

"Just routine," I said, "so we can—"

"You found her, didn't you? It's that body they found at the quarry... Oh my God, Jasmine, she's dead!"

"No, *no*," I said. "We don't know that."

"But that's why you're here," the girl was sobbing, tears streaming down her cheeks. "You think it's her; you think it's Jasmine!"

Oh, shit... we need to get out of here.

I knew from experience that sticking around would only make things worse for them. I watched as Tracy slipped the ten-cards into their protective covers and put them away.

"Well," I said. "That should do it, for now. We'll be in

touch. In the meantime, if you think of anything that might be of help, please give me a call."

I handed Thomas one of my cards. "That has my cell number on it. You can call me anytime. Any time at all."

"What about Hawkins?" he grumbled. "You gonna talk to him or not? 'Cause if you won't, I sure as hell will."

Oh, double shit. That's the last thing I need...

I drew myself up to my full height and tried to look commanding. Being almost six feet tall has its advantages. "Yes, I will interview him. No, you will *not*, under any circumstances, talk to Mr. Hawkins yourself. Is that clear, Mr. Thomas?"

He scowled, but nodded.

"Good. I'll call you as soon as I know something." I jerked my head at Tracy. "Let's go."

I walked out without looking to see if Tracy was following. Once in the cruiser, I slammed the door and turned in my seat to face him.

"Okay, Detective Tracy. Let's have it. What's on your mind?"

"Not a thing, Sergeant. Not a damn thing."

"Okay, then: we're done. I don't have to work with a partner I can't get along with, and I won't. You don't talk, you make no effort to help, and you have no insight to offer. I might as well work alone. So," I hit the starter, "we'll go back to Headquarters. I'll go see the chief, and you can go back to Narcotics."

I put the car in drive and headed for Bonny Oaks.

"Now just a damn minute..."

The words had barely left his lips when I slammed on

the brakes. If he hadn't been wearing his seat belt he would have hit the windshield.

"Yes, Detective?"

"Look," he said. "I understand you just lost your partner, but I don't appreciate you taking it out on me."

"I'm not taking anything out on you. I just need for you to act like a professional police officer and pull your weight. I don't want to have to tell you to do everything. Use your initiative. Open your mouth now and again."

I glanced sideways at him. He was staring at me. I shook my head. "What?"

"You embarrassed the hell out of me in front of everyone this morning," he said. "Why did you do that?"

I laid it out for him, "You have a reputation."

"What? What have you heard?"

"You really want to know?"

"*Yeah*, I really want to know."

"I've heard you're a first-class asshole. You think women are idiots, good for only one thing. You're a grab-ass, can't keep your hands to yourself. That enough? I have plenty more."

He stared at me, his mouth half-open, but either he didn't know what to say, or he did but didn't dare say it.

"Look, Tracy, I've worked damn hard to get where I am, and I don't take any shit from anyone, especially my partner. I've never worked Narcotics; it must have been tough. But you're here now, and this is a different kind of tough. That 'screw you,' hard-ass attitude of yours won't cut it with me. And another thing: a joke now and then is fine, but I won't tolerate any of your sexual innuendo or harassment. Not. Any. You got it?"

His brow was a field of furrows, his eyes were narrowed, his lips clamped together.

Uh oh! Here it comes.

But it didn't. Suddenly his features softened, and he looked at me with sad-puppy eyes worthy of a velvet painting.

"You know, Sergeant, I think I do. It may take a while but I promise, I'll work on it." Then he folded his arms, laid his head back against the headrest, and closed his eyes, a slight smile on his lips.

Son of a bitch. He's trying to play me! Okay, buddy: game on.

CHAPTER 4

HENRY'S TIRE SHOP WAS ONE OF THOSE NASTY, oily little places that do more business in used tires than new; that and general shade-tree mechanic work.

And if you trust them with your vehicle you deserve all you get.

Henry himself was more biker than mechanic: tattooed arms and neck, weather-beaten face, and a leather vest emblazoned with a Harley logo. He was lounging outside the office door in a beat-up old leather recliner, a beer in one hand, a cigarette in the other. He squinted up at me through bleary eyes.

"Well, lookey here," he said, lifting the hand with the smoke to shade his eyes. "If you ain't a sight for sore eyes, I dunno what is. What can I do you for... Ah." He had recognized the white unmarked car for what it was. "Cops. What d'ya want?"

"I'd like to talk to Joe Thomas. Is he here?"

"Hey, Joe," he shouted. "Lady cop here wants you."

Joe Thomas was not at all like his brother. He was

younger by at least ten years; I figured him to be about my age. Maybe a little older. Tall, close to six feet, long blond hair held back by a red and green doo-rag, arms tattooed from shoulder to wrist. He must have worked out, a lot. Even through the sweat-soaked t-shirt, the well-defined six pack and pecs rippled as he moved.

If this man's not on steroids...

He came out of the shop wiping his hands on an oily rag, which he then stuck into one of his belt loops.

"Yeah. What d'you want? This about Jasmine? You found her?"

"Maybe," I said, flashing my badge. "I'm Sergeant Gazzara; this is Detective Tracy. Can we have a word, in private?"

He nodded. "C'mon through. We can use the office, right, Henry?"

Henry nodded, squinting up at me under the shade of his hand, the cigarette ash almost down to his knuckles.

"You said maybe?" Joe asked, as he sat down on an old car seat. I looked around. There was nowhere else to sit, other than behind the great man's desk. "The girl they found in the quarry, right? It's her?"

"As I said, maybe. We haven't yet identified her, which is why I'm here. We collected prints from Jasmine's bathroom, which we hope will tell us yes or no. I need your prints so we can eliminate them."

"From her bathroom? I don't go in there. Why do you need mine?"

I looked hard at him. "I just told you. To eliminate them—"

"Yeah, but," he interrupted me, "I told you I don't go in there. So I don't see why."

"Are you refusing to provide them, Mr. Thomas?"

He shrugged, "I don't see any point in you having them. So yeah, I guess I am."

"Now, why the hell would you do that?" Tracy said, stepping forward while entering a number on his cell. "You got something to hide?"

Before Thomas could answer, Tracy had his phone to his ear. After a moment, he said, "Yeah, it's me. I need to know if there are any warrants out on a Joseph Thomas. He lives on..."

"Okay, okay," Thomas said, rising to his feet. "Keep your friggin' hair on. You can have my prints. I just didn't see any need, is all."

Tracy grinned and slipped the phone back in his pocket.

Okay. That's another point for nerve. He might not be utterly hopeless.

Tracy took Thomas's prints while I continued to question him, though at this stage I couldn't ask much without blowing my chances for a more in-depth interview later. I needed a positive ID first.

I agreed with Tracy on one thing: Thomas probably had something to hide. The guy had that shifty 'I don't want to talk to you' look about him.

"When did you last see Jasmine?" I asked.

"Shit. How the hell should I know? Weeks ago, I guess. The night she went missing?"

Why the hell do some people insist on answering a question with a question?

"That would have been Friday, the eleventh?" I asked, checking the calendar in my phone.

"Yeah... I guess... I dunno. Might have been the night before. I don't always get outta here on time, like. She's a wild one, likes to be out with friends, or whatever."

"Whatever? What does that mean?"

He shrugged, "Nothin'. She's like all kids her age. Don't like being told what to do. You know. Cletus and Arlis, they ain't the strictest parents. All kids needs a whuppin' now and then. Keeps 'em in line. Didn't do me no harm. Jasmine's... well, she does what she wants, mostly. Michael too. Sophia, not so much, but she's the baby. You know how that goes, right?"

With a 12-year gap between me and my older sister, I had essentially been an only child. So, no, I didn't know how that went. But I let it pass.

It was on the tip of my tongue to ask where he was the night Jasmine was abducted, but I didn't. For one thing, I wasn't investigating the missing girl case. Not yet, anyway. For another, I wanted to identify the girl in the morgue and get a more accurate time of death before I started asking about alibis. Doc had called while we were on the road to tell me that Dr. Wu was already on his way and would be arriving at the forensic center around three-thirty that afternoon.

Tracy had wrapped up his work and put away the ten-cards with Thomas's prints, so I just nodded and told him thanks and goodbye. We'd leave the full interview for another day, if and when it was needed.

As we walked to the cruiser, I looked at my watch. It

was almost three o'clock. I suddenly realized I hadn't eaten since before eight that morning; I was ravenous.

"I need something to eat, Detective," I said to Tracy as I pressed the starter. "I'm thinking something quick and easy. How about you?"

"Sounds good to me. You want a burger or... what?"

"No, something lighter, a salad, I think. Then we'll head back to forensics. Dr. Wu should be there soon. Wendy's drive-through?"

He shrugged by way of agreement.

Wow. Such enthusiasm.

I threaded the car through the heavy traffic heading north on I-24 toward the Ridge Cut.

CHAPTER 5

Doctor Jason Wu was something of an enigma. I'd met him before, a couple of times. An extremely intelligent Asian-American man, medium height, frighteningly thin, quiet almost to a fault. Even when offering his opinion, he had to be prodded and pushed, preferring to put his thoughts on paper rather than provide them verbally. That day, I intended to push him. First, I'd had to get back to the department and hand in the latents and ten-cards to Margo Harris, our resident fingerprint expert; it was almost three-forty-five when we walked into Doc Sheddon's den.

Doc was leaning with his back against the stainless-steel sink at the foot of the autopsy table, his arms folded across his chest, peering over the tops of his half-glasses as he watched Wu work. Carol Oats had taken up a similar position on Doc's left—yin and yang if ever I saw them.

Tracy asked if he could stay out in the waiting room. I said he could. There was little to learn from Wu other than a more precise time of death, and even that was doubtful. From what I knew of forensic entomology, the outside temperature was a huge factor when considering the activity of the insects, eggs, and larvae that infested a decaying body. So, knowing how high the temperature was inside the pipe, I had my doubts as to how close the good doctor could get to an accurate PMI.

He looked up as I entered the autopsy room, acknowledging my presence with a slight nod. "Sergeant," he said. Then he returned his attention to the work at hand... said hand inserted deep in the victim's abdomen, Carol's neat stitching now in tatters.

I took my stand at Doc's right side; together, we watched as Wu lifted sample after sample from the cavity and inspected them through a huge round magnifying glass before transferring tiny samples to slides and then to the microscope. And all the while, not a word passed his lips.

Doc glanced sideways at me, smiled, shook his head and shrugged. "He's thorough. I'll say that for him," he whispered in my ear.

Wu looked up at him, cocked his head to one side. "I heard that, Doctor Sheddon," was all he said, as he returned to his minute examination of a fat white maggot that squirmed and wriggled in the grip of his tweezers. The bend of his back, the cocked head, the fierce concentration, all reminded me of a buzzard pecking away at...

Oh, Lord, don't go there...

Finally, he stepped away from the body, stripped off his gloves, and doused his hands liberally with cleanser from a dispenser on the wall. He took up his iPad, flipped through several screens until he found what he wanted, tapped rapidly on the screen, and then laid it down again.

"Doctor Sheddon," he began. "You estimated the time of death as being sometime between the sixteenth and eighteenth of the month. That must have been difficult for you, considering the advanced state of putrefaction. Would you care to enlighten me as to how you arrived at that finding?"

Sheddon colored slightly. He wasn't used to having his work questioned, and Wu sounded like an unforgiving professor.

"I arrived at my finding *because* of the advanced state of decomposition. Under normal circumstances, in a more temperate environment, I would have placed the PMI at three to four weeks. However, on testing the morning, midday, afternoon, and evening temperatures inside the pipe, and finding the range to be extreme, I decided the stage of decomposition we see now could, and probably would, have been reached in a much shorter time: eight to ten days."

"Yes. Well, I disagree with you, slightly. My own estimate is that she died seven to eight days ago, sometime between eight o'clock on the evening of the twentieth and ten the following morning."

Doc looked sideways at me and winked, but said nothing.

He's thinking about that sausage biscuit, I just know it.

"Infestation," Wu continued, "begins within minutes of death. That being so, she must have been exposed to the elements when she died. The accelerated putrefaction is, as you say, due to the high temperatures to which the body was subjected."

Wu returned to the examination table. "As you see, the larvae of lucilia sericata..." he paused and looked at me, then said, "the common green bottle fly, are fully developed. Some, unable to find a more suitable place to pupate, have already done so within the body."

"So, Dr. Wu," I said. "Just to be sure I fully understand, you're saying she died just seven days ago, not ten. You're sure?" I knew as soon as I asked the question I was in trouble. You don't question experts in their field.

"Of course I'm sure," he snapped. "Now. If we're done. I need to get back to Knoxville. Do you have any... *legitimate* questions before I leave?"

I smiled sweetly at him, "Yes, Doctor. I do. Dr. Sheddon thinks she was killed mid-morning. That would mean, according to *your* findings, that she died on the morning of the twenty-first, perhaps even as late as ten o'clock. Do you agree?"

"Excuse me?" He looked at Sheddon. "Please explain how you came to that conclusion."

And he did. And Wu stared at him, nodding slowly.

"Ye-es," he said, somewhat reluctantly. "That could be a factor. Circumstantial, of course, but a factor. Perhaps. If that's all?" And away he went.

I was excited. Never once did I expect to be able to tie the time of death down so precisely.

"Okay, Doc," I said. "I'm calling it between eight and noon on the twenty-first. You agree?"

He shrugged, then said, "If what he said is accurate, then yes. Go for it. If he's wrong, though, or if I am... well, you know the consequences."

"Aw, c'mon, Doc. This is the best possible news! Don't be such a spoilsport."

"Okaaay... but..."

"But what?" I asked, still smiling.

"I'd run it by Harry if I were you. He has a nose for these things, and—"

I don't believe it. Even Doc?

I had known I'd face skeptics, of course I would. Harry's a force of nature, so I was rarely the center of attention during an investigation. Seeing me alone, people were bound to wonder if I could run the whole show. Hell, I wondered the same thing myself.

But Doc knew me better than most. He knew I pulled my own damn weight. This was a surprise. I had to admit, if only to myself, it hurt.

"Are you saying I'm not up to it?" I asked, still half-joking.

"No, not at all. But as they say, two heads, right?"

I nodded, mentally crossing my fingers. "I'll do that." *When hell freezes over.* "Before I go though, let me run something by you."

"Okay."

"She was killed mid-morning on the twenty-first. But Wu said she was exposed to the elements. Killing her outdoors in broad daylight seems pretty unlikely."

He nodded, thoughtfully.

"So, I'm thinking the crime scene has to be somewhat private. But it can't be completely closed off, or else the flies couldn't get to her. Right?"

He looked skeptical. "Yes and no, I suppose. Those little suckers will find a body within minutes in the open air, but even in a closed environment, they'll find it sooner rather than later. And if she was dumped in that pipe soon after death—"

"Right, but if you and Wu are sure she was killed midmorning on the twenty-first, it's a strong bet she wasn't dumped until after dark, so again the question is, where was she? She was still alive ten days *after* she was abducted. She was held somewhere for *ten* damn days. Where?"

"Ah, when you find the answer to that question, you'll also find your killer, I think."

I was on a roll. "And he went out and got her breakfast less than an hour before he killed her. That just doesn't make any sense! What kind of person does that?"

He shrugged, pushed himself away from the sink, took a couple of steps toward the autopsy table, and looked down at the girl's face. "Who knows?" he said, more to her than to me. "What kind of person does this?"

He sighed, turned away from the table, and said, "Lilo will be here later this afternoon. He'll make her a little more presentable, but I would try to keep the parents from seeing her, if you can." He looked at his watch. "Well, Kate. You know how to reach me." He stuck out his hand.

I shook it and thanked him. Then I went out into the lobby to collect m'man Tracy. I found him reading a gun magazine.

"Well?" he asked.

"Between eight AM and noon on the twenty-first."

"Whoa, that close? He's good!"

I smiled, "Well, it wasn't all him. It was Doc who tightened it up..."

My phone rang. I looked at the screen. It was Margo,

and my heart skipped a beat. The moment of truth had arrived.

"Hey, Margo. You have good news for me?"

"I do. We have a match. The prints you gave me match those of the victim."

I smiled grimly. "Thanks, Margo. I owe you a beer. I need you to dust the kid's room, but we should let the family know before you go busting in there. I'll have Detective Tracy go talk to them and let them know you're on your way, okay?"

"Yeah, that's okay. But considering the overtime, you owe me a scotch, is what you owe me."

"Fair enough. Talk to you tomorrow morning."

I turned to Tracy, "It's her. It's Jasmine Thomas." I looked at my watch. It was almost six. I was tired and in no mood to face the Thomases that evening. I needed to think...

Well, Dick wanted Homicide; a little trial by fire might not be the worst thing.

"Go tell the family the bad news, Detective Tracy," I said, quietly. "Just the facts, no more. And tell them they need to let Margo Harris dust Jasmine's room for prints."

I paused. Then I said, "Look at me." He did. "They cannot see her. Not yet. If they ask, make some excuse. If they insist, tell them I'll arrange something. Got it? Good. Meet me in the office at eight-thirty tomorrow. Don't be late."

He looked put out, but he nodded. I dropped him off in the PD parking lot and left him to it.

I didn't bother to go into the office myself. I'd had enough. I wasn't in the mood to go home either, so I made the call.

"Harry. You home? I'm on my way. I need a big ol' hot bath, a glass of wine, and spectacular dinner. You up for that?"

Yeah. Harry was up for that.

CHAPTER 6

Harry was in the kitchen when I arrived.

Thank God.

He had wild rice cooking and two slabs of salmon ready for the grill. The bath was waiting, and he had just uncorked a very drinkable Riesling. I swilled down a half glass, held it out for a refill, then headed for the bathroom.

I threw some salts into the bath, put my hair up, stripped, stretched. I turned on the whirlpool jets, and then gently lowered myself into the steaming water, lay back, and closed my eyes. For what must have been all of ten minutes, I lay there and let the water wash away all my cares and woes, and then...

"Hey, you gonna lie there all night?"

I jumped. Harry was standing over me, towel in hand.

"Oh, m'God, Harry. Just go away and let me drown, okay?"

"Nope. Not okay. The rice is done, the grill's hot, and I'm starving. Now get your fat ass out of there and let's eat."

"Fat ass? *Fat ass?* What fat ass?" I hauled myself up out of the water and turned my back to him, so that he might check it out. I twisted round, looked at him over my shoulder. He was grinning like a baboon.

Do they grin, baboons? I wonder...

"Yeah," he said. "Nice and fat."

I spun around, wrapped my arms around him, and cut him off with a kiss, long and hard.

"Fat, my ass," I said when I came up for air. "Now, just look at you. You're all wet and... Oh, but you just want to eat, right?"

"Right," he said, lifting me bodily out of the tub. "But right now, salmon isn't on the menu. You are."

And I was.

It was after eight when we finally sat down to eat. I was more worn out than relaxed, tell you the truth, but I will say this: Harry Starke sure knew how to turn me into a shivering pile of leftovers.

I sat down while he threw the salmon on the grill, then he joined me. I was in one of his t-shirts, and well into my third glass of Riesling. He was wearing a tee and boxers, sipping on a large glass of very expensive scotch.

How does he drink that nasty stuff?

The salmon was out of this world; the rice, by then, had been cooked down to mush. Even so, it hit the spot, and I was in one of those moods where nothing mattered but the moment.

We left the dishes to fend for themselves and went into the living room, to the huge sofa Harry had set in front of a vast, floor-to-ceiling picture window. Harry's favorite spot on earth and, I guess, mine too. At least it was in those days.

I met Harry when I was just out of the Police Academy. That was in 2000; I was twenty-two, he was thirty. And rich as hell, though you'd never know it. His mother had died a couple of years earlier, leaving him a small fortune in property and investments; he's more than tripled it since.

After I'd spent a couple of years in uniform, I was assigned to Harry as his partner. It was one wild ride, right up until he quit. Now he runs a very successful private investigation agency in Chattanooga.

Harry's big. Six-two, rugged, fit as hell. He's witty, and smart—bordering on genius, I think, though he'd deny that. Harry has a conscience... and a dark side. He will, without hesitation, hurt you if he has to.

He also has this weird sort of sixth sense thing going on. I never have really gotten a handle on it, but it's there. It's not that he speaks with dead people, but if you told me they follow him around, I wouldn't be a bit surprised.

And he's like a damn dog with a bone. He never lets go. He's a great detective, teacher, mentor, and lover. There are times, even today, when I miss him.

We had something special, did Harry and I. Too bad he blew it. His loss. But in a funny way, Amanda's gain. He's changed a lot over the years. We both have. I think it's for the better.

That night, we sat together and gazed out at the Tennessee river. I remember there was a full moon. The surface of the water was a field of glittering silver, the soft glow of the lights on the Thrasher Bridge reaching toward us like golden fingers. The mood lasted for... oh, I don't know, maybe thirty minutes. And then he broke it.

"So," he said, quietly. "How was your first day without me? You going to be able to cope?"

Oh, for the love of God...

"It was *fine*; long, but fine. You know how it is."

He nodded, "Anything you want to run by me?"

"Uh... no." *No!* "Not that I can think of, why?"

"Just trying to be helpful. This is, after all, your first case as the lead, and if I can help in any way, you only have to ask."

I nodded, but said nothing. I wanted to stand on my own two feet; I had to be able to make it without him. And that's a paradox. Today, I have no problem bringing him in to help with a case. I've been doing it for years. It's now gotten to the point where Chief Johnston expects to find him working difficult cases with me. But then? I was going to find Jasmine's killer, and with no help from Harry Starke.

I changed the subject. "Hey, guess what! I have a new partner."

"Whoa. That didn't take long. Anyone I know?"

"Oh, yes. You know him. It's John Tracy."

I could see by the look on his face that he didn't know whether to laugh or just stay quiet; he chose neither.

"Oh boy." He shook his head. "That's not good. I'm sorry, Kate."

"Don't be. I can handle him."

"He was at the academy with me," Harry said. "Smart as a whip, but no drive. His mouth has a bad habit of running away with him, which is why he spent all those years in Narcotics. You'll have to lead him around by the nose."

"I already figured that out," I said, and proceeded to tell him about my... inspiring meeting with Detective Tracy. Inspiring for him, anyway.

By the time I'd finished, Harry was smiling. "Well, I guess it's like you said. You can *handle* him."

I made a face. "No thanks. One and done."

Harry laughed. He has a great laugh. "So. Jasmine Thomas. You're certain it's her, right?"

I nodded. "It's her; I sent Tracy to break it to the family. I'm wondering now if I might have made a mistake. He was quiet for most of the day, but when he did open his mouth..." I was thinking about the way he'd handled Joe Thomas.

"I wouldn't worry about it," Harry said. "Let him do his thing. You never know. So, are you going to tell me about it, or not?"

I sighed. "It's not going to be easy. I'm starting out cold. She was abducted weeks ago, on her way to the mall. At least I assume that's where she was going. It's what she told her mother. Whatever, she didn't make it, or if she did that's where she was grabbed, if she was grabbed... maybe she knew her abductor, went with him willingly." I was rambling, thinking out loud. Harry just sat quietly and listened. He's good at that; it's what makes him a great detective.

I went on in like manner for several more minutes, finally stopping at the point where I'd gotten the positive ID from Margo. I leaned back on the sofa, sipped on my wine, and stared out at the glistening field of silver and gold.

"Suspects?" he asked.

"The usual. Family first, then boyfriends and wannabes,

neighbors... One neighbor in particular, Russell Hawkins. Jasmine's father thinks—no, he's sure this guy's been stalking her, but I won't know until I interview him. Then there's an uncle. The man is built like a brick whorehouse. I'm sure he's on steroids."

"You want me to help out? I could do some of the—"

"No," I interrupted him. "You've been gone less than three days. How the hell d'you think it would look if you had to come back and rescue me? I'm betting Johnston will be keeping an eye on me."

I snuggled up to him, he put his arm around me, I kissed his cheek. "Thanks anyway."

I lay there in his arms enjoying the moment, then I sat up, linked my hands at the back of his neck, and pulled him to me. His lips tasted of scotch.

Hmmm, maybe I could get to like it...? Nah.

I leaned back and looked at him, my hands still at the back of his neck. "I need an early night. You want to put me to sleep?"

He flashed a wide grin at that. "I wouldn't have put it quite that way, but what the hell, I'd like an early night myself."

Early night, my ass. I was still awake an hour later and loving every minute of it. I know he was too, because eventually I had to put a stop to the fun. After a quick shower together—he does have the nicest hands—I hit the sheets and remembered no more until Harry shook me awake, handing me a cup of steaming black coffee to make up for it.

CHAPTER 7

WONDER OF WONDERS. I ARRIVED AT MY CUBICLE at eight o'clock the next morning to find Dick Tracy waiting for me. Even more shocking was his appearance. Yes, his hair was still too long for my liking, but he had on a brand-new pair of sports pants, a FootJoy golf shirt, and tan loafers, no socks. He looked good, and he obviously knew it, grinning at me as I stared at him.

"Nice, right? Council Fire Golf Club. I can't wear a suit, I've been undercover way too long. But this is ok." He spread his arms, admiring himself.

"You'll do, Cowboy. I thought you had to be a member to shop at Council Fire?"

"Yeah, that's right. I'm not, but my brother is. I bought a half-dozen shirts, three pairs of pants, the shoes, a couple—"

"Fine. Let's get to it. Pull up a chair," I said as I sat down at my desk. He did.

"You went to see the parents last night, right? How did that go?"

"Not good. Mom had a conniption, ended up collapsing. Cletus had to take her to the emergency room. I went with them. They gave her something to knock her out, so I took off. It was pretty bad, Kate—I mean, Sergeant. I don't think I handle that stuff well. I'll try to be a little more gentle next time, if there is a next time..." He stared at me, the open question in his eyes. Clearly, he was hoping I'd decide against a next time. I ignored him.

"Well," I said, "now they know, so we can start filling in some holes. The Thomases are the first stop this morning, then Russell Hawkins, then Joe Thomas.

"We'll need a decent photo of Jasmine, and a list of her friends, especially boyfriends, if she had any. I want her car; give Charlie Peck a call, see if they've found it. I also want CSI to go over her room and bathroom, which the Thomases won't like. I'm looking for a journal. Most kids have some way of venting, even if it's in e-mail or texts with friends. ... maybe she had an iPad, or a laptop. I didn't see one in her room, and that's weird."

He didn't hear me. If he did, he didn't respond. He was talking to the Traffic Commander. I waited.

Finally, he disconnected, "They don't have it. Not yet."

"Damn. They looked at the airport and the malls?"

He nodded.

"Damn," I repeated. "There aren't that many places it could be without being noticed. It should be easy enough to find unless it's in the river, or outside the city limits... I need to call the sheriff."

Sheriff Arnold Crupp was a long-time friend of Harry's, which gave me an in. Yes, I was prepared to use Harry's name from time to time; no, that didn't count as getting help. What's the point of having friends if you can't drop their names now and again?

In this case, I wouldn't have to drop it. Arnie knew me almost as well as he knew Harry and, though I wasn't supposed to have it, I had his cell number.

"Hello, Sheriff," I said. "This is Kate Gazzara. You got a minute? I need a favor."

"The hell it is? The hell you do? It's been a long time, Kate. By the way, how did you get my number?"

The truth was, I didn't know, and that's what I told him.

"So, what's the favor? Not that I'm making any promises."

"I know you must have heard about the girl in the pipe, Arnie. Well, I caught the case."

He was silent for a moment, then said, "What do you need."

I knew the man; he would move heaven and earth.

"We can't find her car; a pale-blue Honda Civic, 2005. I was wondering if—"

"Yeah, of course. I'll tell my boys to be on the lookout. If we find it, you want me to call you?"

"That would be good. Thank you."

"I don't have *your* number," he said, sarcastically.

I almost laughed out loud, but I gave him the number instead and thanked him, disconnected, then leaned back in my chair to consider my options. I picked up my phone again and called Margo Harris.

"Hey Margo. I was wondering, how many of those ten-cards matched prints found in Jasmine Thomas's room?"

"All of them. I was just preparing my report. I'll send it

to you as soon as I'm done."

"*All* of them?"

"Yes. They were all taken from family members, correct?"

"Yes, that's correct."

"So yeah, they were all in there at one time or another."

"Thanks, Margo."

I wasn't expecting that. Now I had some thinking to do. So, I did. Then I called Detective Sarah Foote.

"How's it going, Sarah?" I asked.

"Going is about all I can tell you right now. We're still working the door-to-door. There are a lot of residences up there."

"Just the ones bordering the quarry site is all we need for right now," I said.

"Yeah, I know that, and that's what we're doing. There were a lot we couldn't speak to yesterday; either they weren't home or just not responding. So, we're on our second go-around, trying to contact the ones we didn't get in touch with yesterday."

"Any idea when you'll be done?"

I could almost see her shaking her head, "Sometime early this afternoon, I hope. In the meantime, if I find anything I'll call you. Oh, we have found three unofficial entrances to the site. Just trails, well hidden. If you didn't know they were there, you'd never see them. Two of them lead off from back yards, one on Aston, the other on Lord, and guess what?"

"Those are two of the houses where you didn't get a response," I guessed.

"Yeah, but the house on Lord is vacant, locked up tight.

I have two officers searching the yard and the trail; so far, nothing. The other house, the one on Aston, is occupied, but they must be at work or something. I dropped by last night, just after nine, but the lights were out and nobody answered the doorbell. I'll keep trying. The third trail is a narrow track that leads directly through the trees from Ridgecrest Drive to the quarry. It looks like it's used pretty often. There's just room enough to walk on it. I'd say that's the one the kids use. Speaking of kids, I have a couple of names. You want them now, or later, when I get back to the office?"

"Later is fine—I need to go talk to the family. You know we got a positive ID on the body, right?"

"Yeah, I heard. Good luck with that. I'll see you at the office this afternoon, around two-ish?"

"Yes. If anything comes up, I'll let you know."

I sat and thought for a minute, then I called Margo Harris again. She picked up on the first ring.

"Margo," I said. "Sorry to bother you again, but there's something I need to know."

I asked the question. She told me what I needed to know. I disconnected, leaned back in my chair, closed my eyes, and took a moment. I let the buzz of muted conversations float past; the place never was really quiet, not even at night.

I thought about Jasmine, wondered what she'd been like.

Joe Thomas said she was wild. Loud and sassy, I bet. A kid without a care in the world.

I opened my eyes. Tracy was watching me expectantly.

I stood, "Let's go see the Thomases."

CHAPTER 8

WE ARRIVED AT THE HOUSE ON WICKMAN LANE at five past ten that morning. The front door opened even before we were out of the car and Cletus Thomas came out to meet us.

"I want to see her. Me an' her mom; we want to see Jasmine. We have a right, and you can't stop us."

"You're right, Mr. Thomas. I can't stop you, nor would I, but it's not a good idea. Not until the undertaker has made her look..."

Oh shit...

"Has made her look presentable."

"Screw you, Detective. I want to see her—"

"Here," I said, interrupting him, and flipping the lock screen on my phone. "Take a look, and then tell me if this is the way you want to see her, or your wife for that matter."

I pulled up the autopsy picture I had taken and said I wouldn't use unless I had to. Well, I had to. I had to shut it down before Mrs. Thomas entered the argument."

"Oh, Jesus Christ," he gasped. "Oh shit, oh my God, my poor baby girl."

He was gasping for breath, his chest shuddering.

"Okay. *Okay,*" he blurted. "Put it away. If Arlis sees that she'll, she'll, she'll... Oh, my God. I'm gonna kill the mother f—"

"Stop," I interrupted him again, as I slipped the phone into my pocket. "Don't say something you'll regret. We don't know who killed—"

"Hell yes you do!" he shouted. "I told you who done it. That piece o' crap Hawkins done it. When're you gonna arrest him?"

"Calm down, Mr. Thomas. We're doing all we can to catch the person who did this, and we will. I promise."

"Yeah, right, just like all the other murders that have gone unsolved in this damn town. You'll spend a couple days screwin' around, then you'll shove it on a shelf somewhere and forget about her. Just like you always do."

"That's not going to happen. I'll find the person who did this and we'll put him away."

"Put him away... put, him, away?" He was shaking his head, his chin almost on his chest. Then he raised his head, and looked me straight in the eye. "You'd better get to him first." Involuntarily, he glanced up the lane toward the Hawkins house "Because if you don't, I'll put him away. I'll bury the son of a bitch alive, is what I'll do."

And I could tell, he would do just that. Or worse. I could also tell he really did believe that his neighbor was responsible for his daughter's death.

I looked over my shoulder. I could just see the southern corner of Hawkins's roof poking up above the trees.

My next stop, I think.

I looked at Tracy. He remained standing beside the car door, watching Thomas. There was no telling what he was thinking.

I heaved a sigh and followed Cletus Thomas into the house. The family was waiting for us, all of them, including both children and Uncle Joe.

The boy, Michael, sat white-faced beside his uncle on the sofa. Sophia was seated at the table beside her mother, Arlis, who was in a state of near collapse.

"I want to see her," she said.

"No, you don't," Cletus said, putting his arm around her. "It's best we remember her as she was, not as she is now. Trust me, Arlis. You don't want to see her."

She burst into tears and buried her head in her husband's chest. Joe Thomas sat rigid on the sofa, clenching and unclenching his fists, his face an angry mask. I looked at him and shook my head. He glared back at me, his eyes mere slits, his jaw set.

"I'm sorry," I said. "I know this is a very bad time, but I have to ask you some questions. Do you have somewhere I can talk to each of you privately?"

Cletus was clearly offended. "Privately? What the hell are you talkin' about? Whatever you've got to say, you can say it to all of us. We ain't got nothin' to hide."

"I know that," I said, gently. "You'll all tell it like it is, but I need to do it one on one; it's protocol."

"Protocol my ass!" But he pushed past me toward a door off the living room. "I use this room as an office. Don't friggin' touch anythin'. Y'hear?"

"I hear, and we might as well begin with you, Mr.

Thomas. The rest of you... if you don't mind waiting, please. I'll be with you as soon as I can."

I let Cletus take his own seat at the table he used as a desk. I sat down opposite him, Tracy pulled up a chair next to me.

I glanced at Tracy. His face was a mask. I knew he was used to interviewing suspects, so I intended to make use of him. I'd already told him on our way over what I was looking for. He was to follow my lead, and jump in whenever he wanted to, within reason.

I opened my iPad, took a small digital recorder from my pocket, turned it on, and set it down on the table in front of Cletus Thomas.

He stared at it, wide eyed, as if he thought it might rear up and bite him.

"If you don't mind, Mr. Thomas, just to make sure we keep the record straight, I'll be recording this interview. It's just a formality to make sure I don't miss anything. Are you okay with that?" I hoped the tone of the statement was soft enough to put him at his ease, because I was going to record it whether he was or he wasn't. Fortunately, he was.

Judging by his demeanor, and how upset he was by his daughter's death, I was reasonably sure he wasn't a suspect, or even a person of interest. Even so, I had to go through the motions, and I knew the first question was going to piss him off big time.

"Okay then," I said. "Let's begin with where you were when your daughter was abducted. That would have been between the hours of seven o'clock on July 15th and eight the following morning."

Well, he didn't blow up, as I had expected him to. Instead, he just nodded. "I was here all night, from just after five when I got in until I left for work at six the next morning. Ask Arlis. I was with her the whole time."

I nodded. It was what I expected, and I believed him. And anyway, it wasn't him I was interested in, or any other member of the family. I wanted to know about Russell Hawkins. So, I asked all the usual questions, heard nothing that set my teeth on edge, made a couple of notes, then leaned back in my chair. I looked him in the eye and dived right in.

"Tell me about Russell Hawkins." And he did. And the more he said, the angrier he became.

"The son of a bitch has been after her for more'n a year," he began. "It begun with him 'bumping into' her at Starbucks, so she said, but that's not how I see it. Bastard was after her. He bought her a coffee an' they sat an' talked for, she said, about an hour. She said they had the same interests. She likes... liked to take pitchers. She has a nice camera, a Nikon with lots o' fiddly bits on it. Never did unnerstand it m'self. Bought it with her tips. She worked part time at Juno's, that's a little restaurant on McCauley, serves country food, biscuits'n gravy an' such..."

He was beginning to ramble. "And Hawkins?" I asked.

"Oh, yeah. Next thing is he's askin' her out. She told him no, but he didn't quit. Wasn't a week went by he wasn't askin'. I caught him watchin' the house, more'n once. An' he was always 'bumpin' into' her in weird places." He made the quote with his fingers. "Like in Penney's, or that Victoria's place, you know. They sells women's underwear. He even approached her in there one time. Said he was lookin' for a present for his sister, only he ain't got no sister, not to my knowledge. Son of a bitch."

"None of that means he killed her," Tracy said. "Just that he's persistent."

"Persistent? You don't know the half of it. He was callin' her all hours of the day an' night, textin' ten, fifteen times a day. She kept sayin' no, but the son of a bitch wouldn't quit."

"And this has been going on for...?" Tracy asked, making a note on his iPad.

"A year. No, more'n a year. It started back in May last year."

"We didn't find a phone, iPad, or laptop in her room," Tracy said, staring him in the eye. "Nor did we find a journal."

"So?"

"So, you're telling me she didn't have any of those things, not even a laptop?"

"Well, she had a phone... she didn't keep no journal, not that I know of. Maybe her mother—"

"So where's her laptop, her iPad?" Tracy persisted.

"She didn't have an iPad, just this." He turned, pulled open a drawer in a filing cabinet, took out a Dell laptop, and laid it on the table in front of him.

"Why do you have it, Mr. Thomas?" I asked. "Did you remove it from her room?"

He shrugged, nodded, then looked up at me, defiantly.

"I just wanted to make sure there was no... crap on it. You know."

"No, I don't know. Tell me."

"I looked through her emails, Facebook, an' such. That's all."

"Why?"

"She's my daughter, for Christ's sake. She was missing. What would you have done? I was just trying find out if... if she was seeing anyone."

"And was she?"

"No. Not that I could tell. There's a bunch of emails from him up the lane, an' a whole lot of messages on Facebook, some from him, most from girlfriends. I couldn't understand most of it. They speak another language, them kids. Jesus. I dunno. Maybe you can figure it all out. I can't."

"I'll need to take it with me," I said.

"Sure. Her phone... it ain't here. I called it. Nothin'."

"Tell me about her," I said.

"What's to tell? She was a decent kid, never no trouble. Did as she was told, mostly. Home by ten. Late sometimes, but no more'n fifteen or twenty minutes. She was a good girl..."

He was a hard man, I could tell, but at that moment there were tears in his eyes, and I knew I'd get little more from him. It was time to let him go.

"Okay, Mr. Thomas. That'll do for today. If I need you, I'll call."

"Now just you wait a goddamn minute, Missy. What about Hawkins? You gonna arrest him or what?"

"Arrest him? No. Not without cause. I am going to talk to him. Right after I leave here, if he's home."

"I wanna know what he has to say. You'll tell me, right?"

I sucked in my breath and shook my head, "No. I can't do that, Mr. Thomas. But as soon as I have any results, you'll be the first to know. That's a promise. Now, if you don't mind, I'd like to talk to Mrs. Thomas. Would you send her in, please?"

Reluctantly, he rose from behind the table and made his way to the door, which he opened.

"Arlis. They wanna talk to you." And without a backward look, he walked through the living room and out the front door.

"What do you think?" I asked Tracy as we waited.

"About that guy? Nothing. He's clean. Better watch him, though. I've seen that look before; he's about to snap. I wouldn't put it past him to go after Hawkins."

I nodded. He was right. The man was wound tight.

ARLIS THOMAS'S eyes were red from crying, but she held herself erect, obviously trying to hold it together.

"Please sit down, Mrs. Thomas." She did. "I'd like to know about Jasmine—"

"She was a good girl," she interrupted me.

"Yes, I know that; your husband told me. But you're her mother. Girls talk to their mothers. How did she seem in the days before she was...? Did she seem to have anything on her mind?"

"No. Nothin' but her job. She liked that, waitin' tables. She liked the money, the tips, liked to shop. She was happy."

"Did she say where she was going that night?"

She nodded, sniffed, then said, "Just to the mall, to meet friends. She didn't say who and I didn't ask her. I trusted her. She was a good girl."

"Did she seem to be worried about anything? Was she depressed, happy, excited, what?"

She thought for a moment, then said, "Happy and excited, both."

"Why would she have been excited, do you think?"

"No," she said. "I know where you're going. She didn't have a boyfriend. I would have known. She would have told me."

"Are you sure? She was a pretty girl, beautiful, even. Most girls her age are interested in boys... if they don't have one, they want one, have to have one, no matter what. She was dressed..." I had to be careful, "provocatively that night. I think maybe she was dressed to attract attention."

"No. She wasn't like that."

"How do you know? How do you know what she was like when she was with her 'friends?'" I emphasized the word, trying to get my point across.

She sat there, twisting her fingers together, but said nothing.

"Look, Mrs. Thomas. I see it all the time. A boy, maybe even a man, offers a girl a little attention, tells her the things she wants to hear, then one of two things happen: either she goes with him, or she tells him to shove off and he gets mad. Neither one is good. So, I'll ask you again, was she involved with anyone?"

"No! No. If she was, I didn't know about it, but I

would have. She talked to me all the time. We were best friends. She told me everything."

"Did she talk to you about Russell Hawkins?"

She didn't answer, not right away. She seemed to be gathering her thoughts, then she looked at me and said, "Yes, she did. There was nothing going on between them."

She stared at me and I had the weirdest feeling she was lying to me. I looked sideways at Tracy. A waste of time, that was.

Damn, I wish Harry was here. He can read people like no one else.

"Your husband seems to think otherwise," I said. "He's of the opinion that Hawkins was stalking Jasmine. Do you think he was?"

"No. I don't. I think he liked her, and that she liked him, but they weren't... you know."

Yes, I did know, but now I didn't know what to think. Cletus was so sure Hawkins was guilty he was ready to kill him, and might even do it. Arlis, well, I had no idea what she was thinking. I kept waiting for Tracy to jump in, but he didn't.

"Mrs. Thomas. Arlis. Your husband believes that Russell Hawkins killed Jasmine. You obviously don't. Why does your husband think he killed her?"

She sniffed, "They never did get along. Cletus can be... well, you know, obnoxious, when he wants to be. Jasmine was only fifteen when Russell first asked her out. He was thirty-four. Cletus went crazy when he found out. He went up there and threatened to shoot Russell if he so much as spoke to her again. But they're friends, just friends. I asked her if she was... you know, but she said she wasn't. I believed her."

I sighed, looked at Tracy—nothing—then got up, "Can I use your bathroom, please?"

"Of course. There's one next door to this room."

I nodded, "Thank you, Mrs. Thomas. That's all for now. I'll talk to Michael next... Oh, wait. One more question: did Jasmine ever go without... underwear?"

She looked at me, her eyes wide with shock. "No, of course not, she wouldn't! Why do you ask?"

"No reason," I said, with my fingers crossed. "It was just a thought."

She didn't look too convinced, but she nodded, rose from her seat, and exited the room, a broken woman.

I went next door, sat down on the commode, set my elbows on my knees, and put my head in my hands. I felt so out of my depth, so frustrated. I just couldn't read these people, and Tracy... well, he was turning out to be a total waste of skin.

When I got back to the room, Michael Thomas was already seated. I asked him to give us a minute and then I sat and turned to Tracy.

"John, this is not going well. I'm floundering around here by myself. I was hoping for some input from you, but it's not happening, is it?"

"I'm listening, Sergeant, but so far nothing grabs my attention. It's all routine stuff. This is a family in pain. I don't know what else to say, except that this Russell Hawkins intrigues me."

He was right. Maybe I was expecting too much, from him, and from the family.

"Hawkins?" I asked. "Talk to me."

"Jasmine was fourteen when he asked her out. The man was thirty-four. Doesn't that sicken you?"

"Me? Yes. But it's not unusual around here. I know girls who were married at fourteen." I took a breath. "We'll get to Hawkins soon enough. Let's just concentrate on the family for now, ok?"

He nodded.

"Let's get Michael back in here."

Michael Thomas was nineteen and he didn't look like either of his parents, or his sisters. He was more like his uncle in build and demeanor: big, bold, and brash.

I waited until he was seated then said, "Tell me about your sister, Michael."

He cocked his head to one side, narrowed his eyes, frowned. "I dunno what to tell you. I don't know nothin' much. She was three years younger'n me. I didn't hang out with her, not at school nor anywhere's else. She was a good kid, though." He lowered his head and looked away.

"How about boyfriends?"

"Not any that I knows of."

"Were you here the night she went missing?"

He looked up at me, his face was pale, eyes bloodshot, "Yes."

I waited for more. It didn't come.

"And?"

"I was here. She went out, in her car. That's it."

I was slowly shaking my head, frustrated.

"What kind of mood was she in? Worried? Depressed? What?"

He shrugged, "I dunno. I didn't take no notice. I told

you. I didn't hang with her. She did what she wanted. I... I didn't talk to her much. We had nothin' in common."

"How about your friends?"

"My friends? What?" He narrowed his eyes to slits, frowned, looked confused.

"How did she get along with them?"

He slowly shook his head. "She didn't. They didn't... What d'you mean?"

"Did any of them... like her, express an interest in her?"

"Hell, no. She was just a kid, an' my sister. Why would they?"

"You know why, Michael. She was a pretty girl, very pretty, nice figure. You were aware of that, yes?" I watched for a reaction. His head came up and his eyes met mine. He was angry.

"What? What d'ya mean? She was my sister, for God's sake!"

Ah, he knows what I'm getting at. Maybe I hit a nerve.

"Are you telling us that you've never looked at your sister and said to yourself, 'Wow. I'd like to get me some of that?'" Tracy said, sitting up and leaning forward.

Michael stared at him. I watched what was left of the color in his face drain away.

Suddenly, he jumped to his feet. I thought for a minute he was going to take a swing at Tracy, but he didn't.

"You sorry piece o' shit!" he yelled. "She was my sister, an' now she's friggin' dead! What the hell d'you think I am? I oughta knock your friggin' teeth out, is what. Screw you. I'm outta here!" He almost ran from the room, slamming the door behind him.

"Well," Tracy said, grinning widely, "that was informative."

"It was also using a sledgehammer for a thumbtack. Bit much, don't you think?"

He grinned and shrugged. "Hey. You asked for input. In Narcotics—"

"You're no longer in Narcotics," I said, "but I'm not complaining. That was the first real, from-the-heart reaction we've gotten from any of them. Let's get Sophia in here, but take it easy with her; she's still a child."

He nodded and settled back in his seat. I shook my head, got up, and went to get Sophia.

Sophia was a petite little thing. Fifteen years old, though she looked older. From a family photograph on the wall, I could see she was very much like her sister.

I asked all the usual questions, especially about Jasmine's state of mind, but all I got from Sophia was that Jasmine seemed to be happy and almost always in a good mood. They were friends, spent time together in their rooms, did homework together, all of the usual stuff sisters close together in age do—they were just eighteen months apart.

When I asked her if Jasmine had any boyfriends, she said no, and she was quite emphatic about it. Suddenly I had a thought. It seemed to me that everyone we'd talked to so far had said that she wasn't interested in boys... ah, not in so many words, but talking to Sophia....

"Sophia," I said, quietly. "Was Jasmine interested in boys at all?"

"Yes, yes, of course she was. She just didn't have a regular boyfriend."

The answer came quickly. Too quickly. I leaned back in my chair and watched her fidget with her fingers. She looked quickly away, dropped her chin, glanced up at me, then looked away again.

"Sophia, did Jasmine like girls?"

Her head came up, as if she'd been startled, and maybe she had.

"What do you mean? Of course she liked girls. She had lots of friends." And she looked away again.

Oh, m'God. How do I put this?

"Come on, Sophia. You know what I mean. Did she like girls more than boys? Did she like... one girl in particular?"

Sophia looked down at her knees, put her hands to her face, and began to sob.

I waited for her to calm down, then said, gently, "Sophia?"

She looked up, wiped the tears from her eyes with the back of her hand, a defiant look on her face. "Was she a lesbian? Is that what you're asking me? No, she friggin' wasn't!" And with that, she jumped to her feet and flounced out.

"Well, now," Tracy said. "That was a learning experience. So, what are you thinking, Sarge?"

"Don't call me that," I snapped. "I'm thinking that if Jasmine was gay, that adds a whole new dimension to the case. We could be looking for a woman. But that's not something I want to think about right now. I want to talk to Uncle Joe."

Big Joe looked even bigger inside the tiny room. He didn't say a word. He sat down in his brother's chair behind the table, leaned forward, clasped his hands together on the tabletop, and stared at me.

I decided to dive right in. "Last time we talked, Joe, you said," I looked at the note in my iPad, "'She's a wild one, likes to be out, with friends, or whatever.' That's a strange thing to say. What did you mean by it?"

"I told you. Jasmine didn't like being told what to do, and she did pretty much as she pleased. That's all."

"Where were you the night of the eleventh—the night she was abducted—between the hours of seven and midnight?"

He stared at me, a stunned look on his face.

"Am I a suspect?" he asked, slowly shaking his head. "You can't think... Jesus. You can't think I had anything to do with this."

"Where were you, Mr. Thomas?"

He shook his head, "I dunno. I need to think."

He put his head in his hands, then looked up, "I was here until at least seven, I think, then I went out, to Becky's on 153 in Hixson. I needed a new pair of work boots."

"And Jasmine left at... what time?"

He shrugged. "I dunno, six-thirty, six-forty-five. I wasn't payin' no attention."

"So, you arrived at Becky's at, what? It's about fifteen minutes from here, so...?"

"Oh, m'God... seven fifteen?"

"I don't know. You tell me. Did you buy a pair of boots?"

"Yeah, I bought a pair."

"What time was that? How did you pay for them? Do you still have the receipt?"

86

"I dunno what time it was. Around seven-thirty, seven-forty-five, I guess. I paid cash and yes, I have the receipt, somewhere. Why are you questioning me like this?"

I ignored that. "Joe, Becky's closes at eight. I know, because I shop there myself. So you must have been out of there by eight."

"Yeah, okay, I was out by eight. So what? I didn't see Jasmine after she left the house, which was... I dunno, around six-thirty, seven."

"Okay, you went to Becky's," I said. "And you would have been out of there by eight. Where did you go then?"

"Hell, I don't know... Yeah, I do. I went to get somethin' to eat, in Northgate Mall. I had Chinese in the food court."

"So what time exactly did you get home that evening?"

"Screw you, Detective. I don't keep a friggin' time sheet. I just told you, I don't know. Could have been nine-thirtyish, ten. I can't remember. Maybe it was earlier, or later. What the hell does it matter? I didn't kill her, for Christ's sake. Why the hell are you screwin' with me? We all know who done it. That piece o' crap Hawkins at the top o' the lane is who. It's him you should be talking to, not me."

I changed the subject. "When I talked to you yesterday, you were reluctant to provide fingerprint samples. Why was that, Mr. Thomas?"

"I dunno. Just didn't seem right, somehow. I gave 'em though."

"Yes, you did, under pressure. You also said you didn't go into her room, but we found your prints in there. How do you explain that?"

He was getting angrier by the minute, "Listen to me,"

he growled. "You said you took prints from her bathroom. I told you I didn't go into her bathroom. Her bedroom, yes. We all have. You can check my room, you'll find her prints in there. We were friends, dammit. We talked, sometimes in her room, not often, but sometimes, and in mine. Happy now?"

"Excuse me for a minute," I said. "I need to use the bathroom."

Tracy looked up at me in surprise. He didn't say a word, but I knew what he was thinking: *You just went!*

I went because I needed to call Margo. She confirmed that Joe's prints were present only in the bedroom, not the bathroom.

Damn it!

I went back to the room. "Okay, Mr. Thomas. That's all for now. I will, however, need to talk to you again. Please close the door behind you."

"Wait," Tracy said. "I have a question. What exactly was your relationship with your niece?"

He cocked his head to one side, squinted at Tracy. "What... what? What relationship? I was her uncle, for Christ's sake."

Tracy nodded, narrowed his eyes, "You liked her, right?"

"Yeah, I liked her. She was family. Of course I liked her."

"No, I mean you... *liked* her."

He rose to his feet shaking his head, his face white. He started around the desk toward Tracy, then changed his mind and went the other way.

"You sick son of a bitch," he said, quietly. "Know what? Ask that stupid friggin' question in front 'o Cletus or Arlis, and I'll make you wish you hadn't, you piece o' shit!"

I watched the door close behind him, then turned to face Tracy.

"What was that about?" I asked.

"Ah, just jerkin' his chain to see if I could get a reaction. I think he's telling the truth."

"He *is* telling the truth. His prints were not found in the bathroom, but—"

"Okay," he said, "then I'm not sure I understand where you're going with this. He told you the truth about his prints. True, he has no real alibi—Becky's can only confirm the time he bought the boots. But ask me what I was doing two weeks ago and I couldn't tell you either. I believe him. You don't really think he's a suspect, do you?"

I shrugged. "Maybe."

The truth was, I really didn't. He was the kid's uncle and it was easy to see that he was genuinely upset, especially at what Tracy had implied.

"No, I don't," I said, leaning back in my chair and closing my eyes. "I don't have *any* suspects, not yet. It's too soon; way too soon."

He nodded. I rose from my seat and together we went out into the living room where they were all assembled, waiting.

"Thank you for your time," I said. "I'll be in touch." And I turned to walk out the front door.

"Hey, just you wait a damn minute," Cletus said, rising to his feet. "You gonna tell us what's goin' on, or what?"

"Right now, Mr. Thomas, I have nothing to tell you, nor do I expect to have anything for quite a while. The investigation is just beginning. When I have something, you'll be the first to know."

"What about him up the lane?" He jerked his thumb in the direction of the Hawkins home.

I shook my head, exasperated, then turned and walked out the door. Tracy followed me.

CHAPTER 9

WHEN WE LEFT THE THOMAS RESIDENCE, I WAS OF two minds as to what to do next: go interview Hawkins, or go back to the station and talk to Detective Foote. I decided on the latter, mostly because I knew Cletus Thomas was watching from his front window and I didn't want for him to decide to join me.

So instead of turning right out of the driveway, I turned left and headed for Bonny Oaks and then Amnicola. I could interview Russell Hawkins... well, whenever. That turned out to be later the same afternoon.

In the meantime, I called Sarah as I was driving along Bonny Oaks. She was still out working the door-to-door with a half-dozen uniforms, but they were getting toward the end of it.

"Did you find anything?" I asked.

"Not much more than when I talked to you this morning. I did find another one of the kids, so now we have three."

"Well, that's something. Look, leave your guys to finish

up and come on back to the station. We'll go through what you have."

She agreed, so I disconnected and turned my attention to Tracy.

"Any thoughts, John?"

"About the family? Same as before. Look, even I know that the first place you go when looking for suspects is the family. This family? I don't see it. They're all hurting. The only solid lead we have so far is this Hawkins character, and I think we should talk to him, soonest."

I didn't answer. I just stared straight ahead through the windshield. I swung the cruiser right onto Wilder and headed west to Amnicola, lost in thought.

The incident room was quiet, as it usually was at that time of day, just after noon. My storyboard was more fairy tale than novel. Four images of Jasmine Thomas adorned the top of the board: one a recent head shot of the girl, one taken at the forensic center showing the bruising to her neck, and two more taken inside the pipe at the crime scene. Which it wasn't. It was just the dump site. The girl died somewhere else and was then transported to the quarry.

Trace evidence? Physical evidence? I had none of that either. Not yet; I thought that that might change when CSI got through with her clothing.

I added another image of Jasmine to the board. It was one supplied by her mother, a summertime shot of the girl seated beside her sister on a low wall. Where, I had no idea, and it didn't matter. It was a nice image.

I sighed and turned my attention to Tracy, who was standing beside me. He was right about the family. There was no way I could look at any of them as suspects.

"John, why don't you run this Russell Hawkins through the computer, see if he has a record?"

He nodded and left me to it.

Hah, that's a joke. Where the hell is Detective Foote?

I went to my computer, pulled up Google Maps, and printed a map of the Battery Heights area on the large format machine, taking in about a square half-mile of real estate from south of Bonny Oaks to the north of Harrison Pike. I then converted the street map to the Google Earth view and printed that too. I returned to the big board and pinned up the map and the aerial view, then I took a black marker and drew a circle on each one, representing an area some two thousand feet in diameter, a little more than a half-mile.

I stepped back and looked at the map, then turned to look out of the window.

Where the hell is she?

"Hey. Sorry," Foote said. "There's a wreck on Wilder and I got hung up in it."

I nodded, "Go get some coffee. You look like you need it."

"I do. You want one too?"

I thought for a minute, "No. I'm wired enough, and the stuff they make here will kill."

She grinned and hustled off to return a few minutes later with a Styrofoam cup of something steaming, black, and unmentionable.

"Okay, Sarah. Talk to me."

She nodded, opened her iPad on the table, grabbed a piece of paper, and began to write.

"These are the names and addresses of the three youngsters I told you about," she said without looking up from her writing. "According to the two people I talked to, they regularly ride their bikes in the quarry."

She stood up and handed me the paper. I glanced at it, nodded, and handed it to Tracy.

"We'll need to talk to them, John. How about Hawkins? Did you find anything?"

"Nope. Nothing. He's clean."

"Okay," I said, turning to the board. "The quarry is surrounded by a band of dense woodland that varies in depth from a few yards to more than fifty. It can't be seen from anywhere outside of its perimeter, except from the yards of the houses that back up to it. Even then, most of the occupants wouldn't be able to see it without going through thick undergrowth. So, I'm thinking that not many people outside of this circle," I pointed to the map, "would even know it was there."

I paused, stared at the map, then said, "Even the gated entrance is well hidden; it's here, on Bonny Oaks, but you'd never know it."

I flipped the lock screen on my phone and brought up a photo of the quarry's entrance gate and the trail beyond. I printed it, then pinned the eight by ten on the board beside the maps.

"See? You'd never know. That trail hasn't been tended in more than a year; it's almost overgrown. As you can see, it curves away to the right for at least four hundred feet before it reaches the quarry."

"Okay," Tracy said. "So what? It's a great place to dump a body—"

"And whoever dumped her had to know the area, most

likely someone who lived in the vicinity, here." Again, I scrawled a circle over the top of the one I'd already drawn.

"Most of what is inside that circle is Battery Heights, a tight little community, mostly blue collar, that almost surrounds the quarry. And get this," I drew an X on each map. "This is Wickman Lane. This is the Thomas residence and this... is the Hawkins residence."

I took a step away from the board, "Any comments?" I asked.

"Yeah," They both spoke at once, and stopped.

"John?" I asked.

"Hawkins's property backs onto the quarry."

"It does, doesn't it?" I said, thoughtfully. "I want to get a looksee at his property; maybe he has access to the quarry. Okay, what about the kids, Sarah? How do they gain access? You said you had found three places."

"I did. There may be more, but the three I found are here, here, and here. As you can see, two are between homes. They get in through a break in the fence. The other is just a narrow footpath from the road. If you didn't know it was there, you'd never find it." She paused. "None of them are wide enough for anything bigger than a bicycle, Kate."

"Which means the perp carried her in," I said.

Sarah nodded. "He might have brought her to Battery Heights in a car, and then walked her in... but like you said, this is a tight-knit neighborhood. Someone would have noticed a stranger—certainly one carrying a body."

"So," I said, "the perp is probably somewhere inside this circle. We know Jasmine was kept alive for at least five days, but we don't know where. Again, I think it has to be somewhere here." I scrawled another circle over the two I'd already drawn. The maps were beginning to look like spider webs.

"I need to talk to Mike Willis," I said, to no one in particular. "Maybe he's found something we can use."

Mike Willis was our head of CSI operations, had been since long before I joined the force more than six years earlier. He reminded me so much of Harry Morgan. You know, the guy who played Colonel Potter in M.A.S.H.? A weird little man with a brain like a computer, and eccentric? You wouldn't believe. He always seems to be in a hurry. He's short, overweight, and untidy but obsessively clean. Gray hair cut bristly short, bushy eyebrows, and an incongruously large pair of hands. If there was evidence to be found, Mike would dig it out.

He answered on the second ring, but what he had to say wasn't encouraging. In fact, the information he shared provided little more than a forlorn hope. Other than the samples of the fine, dry dirt from Doc Sheddon, and more of the same he found on her shorts and top, nothing. He did, however, agree that it probably came from a dry dirt floor. His best guess? An old barn or shed.

"So," I said. "No fibers, hairs, trace of any kind?"

"The dust had traces of some sort of dried organic material, feces, probably animal droppings, and there are traces of urine, very old."

"Human urine?"

"Eh... I don't think so."

"Hmmm. Okay, Mike. If that's all you have..."

"Sorry, Kate. I wish I had better news."

Me too, I thought as he disconnected.

I sat for minute, thinking, then said to Sarah, "Three vacant properties? You checked them out, right?"

"Yes, two are for sale," she said. "The other is a rental property. It's been vacant for a couple of weeks. There were painters in there when I visited, so I was able to take a look around. There was nothing out of the ordinary. The other two were locked up tight. I'm pretty sure they're clean; you want me to call the realtors and take a look at them?"

"Might as well. It couldn't hurt. Why don't you do that this afternoon? This evening, you can go talk to the kids."

She nodded, rose from her seat, and headed for the door.

I took a few moments to Google Russell Hawkins. I wasn't hoping for much so I was quite surprised when I found more than fifty listings for him.

Must be some other Russell Hawkins.

But it wasn't. The man was thirty-four years old and a writer, a science fiction novelist, quite well-known for his military space operas.

Well, what d'ya know?

I logged out, stood, and said, "Tracy, you're with me."

"Cool," he said. "Where are we going?"

"We're going to talk to our prime suspect... according to Cletus Thomas, that is."

CHAPTER 10

WE DIDN'T CALL AHEAD. I WANTED TO SURPRISE him. I was a little worried about that; it would be a waste of time if he wasn't home. But that wasn't the case. He was home.

Russell Hawkins wasn't what I expected based on the Thomases' assessments. He was an ordinary man, obviously quite wealthy, but ordinary in every other way possible. And deadly boring to boot. He wasn't bad looking, nor was he handsome. At five-ten he was of average height, average build, straight brown hair cut short, with a face you'd be likely to forget the minute you walked away. Dressed in white chinos, a pink short-sleeve shirt, and boat shoes, he opened the door with a smile.

"Can I help you?"

"I hope so," I said. "My name is Sergeant Catherine Gazzara and this is Detective Tracy. We'd like to talk to you about Jasmine Thomas."

"Ah... that. Yes. I heard about that. She was murdered; found in the quarry, so I heard." He glanced over my shoulder in the direction of said quarry. "It's terrible, awful. She was a lovely girl. But, please, do come in. Let's go through to my office. We'll be comfortable there."

His voice was pleasant enough, but he spoke in monotones; I was more than glad I wouldn't have to listen to it for very long.

We followed him into his office; it didn't look like one, it was far too comfortable. Aside from the desk and leather chair, the room was set up for comfort. Expensive furniture faced a large picture window revealing a view of extensively landscaped gardens behind the home. These eventually gave way to the woodlands beyond.

Oh yes, I definitely need to take a look at those.

"There now," he said. "Please, sit down. Can I get you a drink? Something cold, perhaps?"

"No. No thank you," I said, falling back and then sinking deep into a large easy chair. Comfortable? Oh, yes. The best place from which to conduct an interview? No. Still, other than the sofa and two more chairs just like it, there weren't any appropriate seating options. The damn thing almost swallowed me. I looked at Tracy just in time to see him wipe the grin from his face.

"You live alone here, Mr. Hawkins?" I asked.

"I do. My father passed away more than ten years ago—cancer. He was a smoker, bless him. Mom remarried and moved to Florida, the Keys actually, Islamorada. It's beautiful down there. Have you ever been, Sergeant?"

"No—"

"Well, you should go," he interrupted. "Time stands still there. I try to go at least a couple of times each year, if only for a few days. The sea, the white sand, oh, and the fishing. Do you fish, Detective Tracy?" he asked, but went on without waiting for a reply. "The sport fishing is amazing. And, if you stay at the right hotel—which I can recommend, by the way—they'll clean your catch and cook it for you that very same day. You can drive it from here, you know, but it's much better to fly into Fort Lauderdale and drive down from there—"

"I bet it is." Now I was interrupting him, but I needed to get this done, and the drone of his voice was tiring, not to mention annoying. "I'm sorry, Mr. Hawkins, but I'm on a tight schedule. So, if you don't mind, I'll ask my questions and then leave you to whatever it was you were doing."

I heard Tracy snort, then turn it into a cough, but I didn't look at him.

"Of course. Ask away, Sergeant, ask away."

"How well did you know Jasmine Thomas, Mr. Hawkins?"

"Oh, very well, very well indeed. We were friends, you know. Of course, I've known her since the day she was born —well, not quite, but you know what I mean. Over the past couple of years, we became very close. We used to talk together often. Mostly over a cup of coffee at Starbucks, or in the mall."

"Did you ever ask her out?"

"Out... on a *date*? Good God, no, she was half my age! Besides..."

"Besides what?"

"Well, she wasn't exactly my... type?" He raised his eyebrows expectantly.

I waited.

"Oh, for God's sake, Sergeant. I'm gay."

I looked at Tracy. His face was a mask.

"I see," I said. "I understand you're a writer, Mr. Hawkins." He opened his mouth, but before he could speak, I continued. "So, I assume you work here. Do you remember what you were doing the evening Jasmine was abducted? That was the evening of the eleventh."

It was a bit brutal, but efficient. I knew that each question, closed or open, would solicit a long and rambling answer. And I wasn't disappointed.

"Hmmm, the eleventh, now let me think," he put a finger to his lips and closed his eyes. "The eleventh, the eleventh... ah yes, I was out. I was at Barnes and Noble, at Hamilton Place Mall. I had a book signing for my latest novel, *The Rimworld Wars*. I remember because it went quite well. I write science fiction, you know. There was quite a crowd. Not as many as I would have liked, but very gratifying just the same. I signed... oh, I don't know, fifty or sixty books perhaps. And—"

"And what time would that have been?" I asked, dreading the answer.

"Well, I was invited to be there a little early, to get things set up, you know."

I looked at Tracy. He had a glazed look in his eyes, but I glimpsed a slight smile on his lips. He didn't look over, but I knew it was for me.

"So that took about thirty minutes, which would have made the time... ummm, seven o'clock?" Hawkins didn't wait for an answer. "Yes, seven. I signed books until about eight-thirty... I think that was about it. Anyway, I know I was out of there by nine. So, six-thirty until nine."

Finally. Oh my God.

My head was spinning. I looked at Tracy, silently pleading. "Detective. Is there anything you'd like to ask Mr. Hawkins?" I said, hopefully.

He cut me a sharp look. By now I think he'd gotten the message, and the question wasn't a rhetorical one.

"What time did you return home, Mr. Hawkins?" he asked.

I cringed, but I was glad to let Tracy have his head. Hawkins claimed he was home by ten that night, having stopped at Carrabba's for a quick meal. By the time he finished answering that question we knew more about that restaurant than even its owners probably realized. My God, how that man could talk, and all in a sing-song droning voice that grated on the teeth worse than fingernails on a chalkboard.

And so it went, for maybe another fifteen minutes. By the time Tracy and I had both had enough, we knew he probably wasn't a suspect. Hell, if he had killed her, he needn't have strangled her; he could have talked her to death.

And so, I looked at my watch, made my excuses, and we left him at the door staring after us as we drove away. And then I had a thought. How the hell I'd forgotten, I don't know, but I needed to take a look at the forest behind his house.

"We have to go back," I told Tracy.

"What for? He sure as hell didn't kill her."

"Probably not, but we need to see what access he has to the quarry—it's just behind his property."

So I turned onto Bonny Oaks, then made a U-turn and retraced the route back to the Hawkins residence. Reluctantly, I pushed the doorbell and waited. He opened the door and looked out at me, surprised, eyebrows raised in question.

"Yes?"

"I'm sorry, Mr. Hawkins. I need to take a quick look out back. Do you mind?"

"Oh, because of the quarry? Of course. I'll come with you."

"No! No, that's okay. Detective Tracy and I need to do this alone, if you don't mind."

"Of course," he said, worriedly, "but if you need anything—"

"I'll be sure to get with you. Which way...?"

"Go to the left side of the house," he pointed, "then go 'round the back and across the gardens. There's a path through the trees. You'll see it."

A path through the trees...

I looked at Tracy. He smiled back at me. I knew just what was going through his mind, because it was going through mine: a path through the trees would provide Hawkins with access to the quarry, and the dump site. If that were so, it would put a whole new light on things.

The walk was easy enough. The path was wide... well, not wide, but there was room enough to push a good-sized wheelbarrow, for example. It meandered for some hundred and fifty feet from the gardens to the edge of the quarry. As we approached, my heart began to race; it was looking good. Then... nah. The path ended at the edge of a steep drop of at least fifty feet, and there was no way down. Neither was there a path to the left nor the right circling around the rim. It was a dead end, no pun intended. If Hawkins killed

Jasmine, he didn't transport her to the dump site via that route.

"Find what you were looking for?" Hawkins was standing at his back door as we emerged from the trees. "If you were looking for a way down into the quarry, all you had to do was ask and I would have told you; there's no access. I think there may have been, some time back, when they were digging down there, but not now. It's a fun place to go and sit, though. You know, when the kids are down there doing their tricks, and oh my, can they do some tricks. I don't know how they do it. It looks so dangerous. But it's quite entertaining. Do you know, those kids can ride their bikes up the slope to the point where it's almost vertical? Then they fall back down, but they somehow manage to twist in the air and land on their wheels, amazing."

We both stared at him. I know my mouth was open, but I didn't dare look at Tracy.

"Well, that's very interesting," I said, walking quickly toward the driveway at the side of the house. "We'll be in touch. Thank you for your time." I couldn't get the hell out of there quick enough. By the time we got back in the cruiser, Tracy was laughing like a fool.

"Don't worry," I said, grinning at him. "You can handle him all by yourself next time, if there is a next time."

"Yeah, right. He didn't do it. He doesn't have what it takes. Besides, he has an alibi. She went missing around seven or seven-thirty, and we know where he was from then all the way to ten o'clock."

"Well, we know what he said, but we still have to check it out. Can you handle that one, Detective?"

"Me? Sure. I can do that." He looked at his watch. It

was just after five o'clock. "You want me to do it today? I can. I don't have anything going this evening."

"Yes, why don't you do that? I'll drop you off at the station and then I'm heading home. I have plans for this evening."

"Hot date?" he asked.

"None of your damn business," I said.

I wasn't about to tell him that I did have a date, with Harry. But hot? Well... it could be, but first the man had to buy me a decent meal. I was starving, and a damn burger wasn't going to get it. I was in the mood for a steak, rare and juicy, with beaucoup French fries and a decent bottle of wine.

It was just after six that evening when I finally left the department and called Harry.

"Hey!" he said, "where the hell are you? Dinner's ready, and spoiling."

"Oh, hell, Harry. I need to go home first. I need a shower in the worst way. I've just gotten out of the forest. God only knows what I've picked up in there."

"You can shower here. I'll put the food in the warmer. I have a nice bottle—well three actually—of Riesling in the cooler. C'mon."

That was all it took, so I did.

CHAPTER 11

HARRY WAS OUTSIDE ON THE PATIO WHEN I arrived. He was sipping on a large glass of that fancy scotch he loves so much, but I was pleased to see the open bottle of wine in the ice bucket.

"Hey," he said, looking round as I slid open the glass doors. "You have a good day?"

I didn't answer, and he sat and watched as I poured a brimming glass of wine and dumped myself down onto the wicker chair beside him.

"I take it that's a no."

"Ah, it wasn't so bad. We got a lot done, I think. Still no clue who killed the girl. The prime suspect has a solid alibi, so that screwed things up. The man's a writer, and he may be an idiot, but he claims he was signing books at Barnes and Noble, for Pete's sake. I have Tracy checking it out, but that's pretty damn solid... I can't believe it was random, Harry, that someone simply snatched her off the street."

"But you can't rule that out, right?"

I pondered that for a minute. "No, I can't, and if that's

what happened, and if it's a one off, I'm not going to find him. You know how it is: no connection, no motive... That type of crime is almost impossible to solve."

He nodded, sipped on his scotch, and stared out over the river. There was a light breeze blowing across the water, raising small waves. The sun was still high but casting shadows on the water, turning it into a vast undulating creature, benign then, but during bad weather it could turn into a beast. I saw none of that. All I could see was the bloated body on Doc Sheddon's autopsy table.

"You're sure the family is clean?" he asked without taking his eyes off the river.

"As sure as I can be without any evidence to suggest otherwise."

He nodded. "Alibis?"

I shrugged. "The girl's parents are not persons of interest. Cletus's brother? It hardly seems likely but, whatever, Tracy is out checking his alibi too. I told him to call me if he found anything. I halfway hope to hell he doesn't; then again... it's my first case, and I need to wrap it up, fast."

"If it *was* random, you're screwed," he said thoughtfully. "But you know, I got to thinking: the gate..."

"Yes, what about it?"

"It was locked, yes?"

"Ye-es...?"

"So what happened to the lock?"

I stared at him, not quite comprehending, then the light went on.

"OH SHIT, Harry! How stupid can I be?"

"I need to talk to Tom O'Mally. He was first officer on the scene. Damn, damn, *damn!*"

I looked at my watch. It was just after seven-thirty. If he was working second shift he'd be on duty. I needed his cell number, so I called Charlie Peck.

"Captain? Kate Gazzara. I need to talk to Tom O'Mally; would you have him call me? You have my number? As soon as he can. Please. Thank you."

It wasn't five minutes later when O'Mally called. I was waiting, tapping my fingers against my glass. I snatched up my phone and flipped the lock screen.

"Hey, Tom, thanks for calling back. Question: you had to use bolt cutters to open the quarry gate, right?"

"Yes, that's right."

"The chain and the lock aren't in evidence. You didn't bring them in from the site?"

"Oh shit! No, Sergeant. I didn't think any more about them. I was too involved in what was going on at the quarry."

"Okay. Think back: what did you do with the lock and chain?"

"Ummm, well, nothing. I cut the shackle and tossed them to one side, in the grass beside the gate. If nobody's picked them up, they should still be there."

"Okay, fine. Now listen to me, Tom. This is important. Did you handle them?"

"Well yeah, but only to grab the chain and pull it off the gate."

"So your prints will be on it?"

"Naw... I was wearing standard-issue Tac gloves, I always wear 'em when I'm on patrol."

Whew! Thank you, God.

"Okay, Tom, thanks. I'll go out there and see if I can find them."

"You want me to go? I can."

"No. That's okay. I'll do it. Thanks, Tom." I disconnected, laid the phone down on the table, and looked at Harry.

"Damn it! I should have remembered that chain. And Tom should have known better."

He shrugged, "We all screw up from time to time."

"Yes, but—"

"Go take your shower. I'll come with you. Dinner can wait. You'll have to drive, though." He held up his now-empty glass for me to see, and grinned. I looked at my own glass. Fortunately, it was still half full. I'd be okay, I hoped.

I told him screw the shower, I'd take that when we got back.

The drive from Lakeshore to the quarry took less than fifteen minutes; we arrived at the gate just a few minutes after eight. It was still quite light, so we had no trouble finding the chain and lock. It was in deep grass beside the left-hand post, sun glinting off the shiny finish. I donned a pair of latex gloves from the trunk of my car and gingerly picked them up. I held them up for Harry to see, smiling at my find. I slipped them into a paper evidence bag, signed off on it, and had Harry witness my signature.

"Okay," I said, brightly. "Let's go home. I need a shower and something to eat—"

"Whoa. Hold on a minute. You're forgetting something."

"I am? What?"

"Come on now, Kate. How long have you been doing this? Think about it…"

I thought, but my mind was blank. I stared at him, slowly shaking my head.

"How long has this quarry been shut down?"

"I dunno exactly. A long time, years."

"The chain, Kate, and the lock. They're brand new."

And then I got it, "Oh, shit. The killer brought the new lock with him. He got in the same way we did: he just cut the old one off."

He smiled, and nodded, "Maybe that's around here somewhere too."

"Harry. I'm not doing too well, am I?"

He laughed. "Give yourself a break, Kate. This is your first case on your own. It's going to take time. You'll get there."

"Maybe," I said, moving the long grass around with my feet.

Oh, m'God, I hope there are no chiggers.

"No maybe about it," he said, joining me.

We searched the immediate area around the gate, and many yards beyond, but found nothing other than a few empty Coke cans.

"I'd say our boy took them with him," Harry said eventually. "But just to be sure, first thing tomorrow, you might want to get a team out here with metal detectors. It's almost too dark to see anything now, so I suggest we go home and relax. You want to?"

I did. I could drop the lock and chain off to Mike Willis in the morning.

The evening was pleasant. The food, though a little

stale by the time we got to it, was wonderful. But I couldn't really relax; I just kept wondering if I was up to the job. The chain? The fact that I didn't even think about it? That was a fundamental mistake, one that Harry never would have made... as he proved by reminding me of it.

"You're quiet," he said, as we sat together watching the lights from the Thrasher Bridge reflect off the river. "What are you thinking about?"

"I'm thinking I can't afford to keep screwing this investigation up. That chain thing," I shook my head, frustrated. "Unforgivable. And I have only two suspects, neither of them viable—"

And smack me in the mouth if, right at that very moment, my phone didn't ring. I looked at the screen, flipped it unlocked. "Hello, John. What is it?"

I listened, I nodded, I listened some more, shaking my head. "No way," I said. I looked at my watch. It was already after ten, and all I had on was one of Harry's tees over my panties.

"John, what the hell have you been doing all night? It's almost ten-thirty... Okay, never mind. Look, it's late, and I'm bushed. I can't think straight. I'll talk to you in the morning." And I hung up on him.

"Damn it!" I said, more to myself than to Harry.

"Bad news, I take it?"

"No, good news, actually. Hawkins doesn't have an alibi after all, and Joe Thomas's is so full of holes it's not even funny."

"Hawkins wasn't at B&N?"

"Oh, he was there all right, just not on that day. Oh,

m'God, Harry. I still don't think it was him. Maybe he just made a mistake, got confused about the days."

"What about Thomas?"

"He said he was at Becky's buying new boots and didn't leave until seven-thirty, or thereabouts. But Tracy checked with them: their receipt is time-stamped at six-seventeen. So, either he's lying or he made a mistake too. I don't see it, Harry. Not either one of them."

"Don't overthink it, Kate. Most killers just aren't that smart."

"I know that!" I spouted off, my frustration showing. "But I don't even have a crime scene, much less a viable suspect. What the hell do I do now?"

"One step at a time, Kate. Go talk to the suspects. You need an answer on the alibis. Are they lying, or did they just make mistakes? Talk to your people. You need to find the crime scene, and that second lock and chain."

CHAPTER 12

THE FIRST THING I DID WHEN I ENTERED THE PD building the following morning was hand over the lock and chain to Mike Willis. The second was to tear John Tracy a new one for not calling me earlier with the news about Hawkins's alibi. Having done that, I felt a little guilty. Even if he had called, I wouldn't have been able to do anything about it: I was out searching the quarry gate area. Still, he should have called.

Next, I put in a call to get Jasmine's phone records. I didn't have her phone, but her records? Yes, I could get those.

Might as well see who she talked to that night, and when.

"Hey, Sergeant. Good morning."

I turned and saw Sarah Foote walking across the room toward me.

"Hey, Sarah. Have a seat; I just need a minute to check my messages." There were several, but only one grabbed my attention: Sheriff Crupp wanted me to call ASAP.

Aha, they've found the car.

I called him, and they had. They'd discovered the Honda in a pond just off Highway 58, close to the Bradley County line. Well, the pond owner had found it. He'd noticed the roof sticking up above the water and had called the sheriff's office. They had already hauled it out and it would soon be on its way to Mike Willis. That boy and his team were going be busy.

Still, there was nothing I could do about it right then: the car was on the road and wouldn't arrive at the garage until sometime after ten. I had other things on my mind, namely faulty alibis.

I hung up the phone and turned to Detective Foote, "What do you have for me, Sarah?"

"I visited both vacant houses yesterday. One of them is a new listing; it's been vacant for less than a week, so we can cross that one off the list. The other... I think we can cross that one off too. It's been vacant since June third, but it was locked up tight and there was no sign of forced entry. It was very clean, inside and out. Sorry."

"There's nothing to be sorry about. That's what we do, eliminate the impossible. So, what about the three kids?"

"Ah, now, there we might have something. I talked to all three of them, with their parents present."

I nodded.

"One of them claimed he hadn't ridden the walls, as they call it, for more than a month. He'd been grounded for stealing candy from the local supermarket. Another had been there the evening they found Jasmine, but he got scared when the kids started shouting about it, and he ran off before the cops arrived.

"Finally, Martin Stewart admitted that he was there too,

but left early, before they found her. He's a cocky little monster. All snot and bravado. He's all of four-six, but he's got an attitude you wouldn't believe. If he was there, I doubt we'll get him to admit it.

"He did have one little nugget for me though. He claims there's often a man watching them from the rim of the quarry. He claims the man was there that day. I asked him if he would recognize him if he saw him again. He said he wouldn't, the man was too far away. Again, I'm not sure I believe him, but it's something, right?"

"Yes, it's something," I said, "and I think I know who it was."

"You do?" she asked, surprised.

"Yes. That would be Russell Hawkins. His property backs onto the quarry, and he watches the kids playing. He told us as much. There's no access from there, so I'm not sure if it helps. Makes me wonder though: was he up there the night Jasmine's body was dumped? Did he see it?"

I leaned back in my chair, linked my fingers together at the back of my neck, closed my eyes, and stayed like that until finally, "Sergeant?"

I opened my eyes, "Yes, Sarah. Sorry. I was thinking, trying to figure out what I was going to say to him. Hawkins. His alibi isn't an alibi.

"John," I said, as he pulled up a seat and sat down beside Sarah.

"I've just come from Mike Willis," he said. "He asked me to tell you that Jasmine's car is on its way to the shop and that he'll get started on it as soon as it arrives. In the meantime, he said to tell you that the lock and chain are clean. Whoever it was must have been wearing gloves. So that's a bust."

"That's a bummer," I said. "I was hoping we'd have gotten some prints. I wonder where the hell the old chain is. Oh, that reminds me. I need to talk to Mike myself."

"Hey, Mike," I said when he picked up. "You have anyone you can spare for an hour, maybe two? No, no. Yes, two would do fine. Have them go search around the quarry gate area with metal detectors. They'll be looking for another lock and chain. My guess is that whoever put the one I gave you on the gate threw the old one away. It could be as far out as ten or fifteen yards, so have them do a thorough search. Yeah? Cool, thanks, Mike. Oh, and, Mike? I'm sending John Tracy back to you. Yes, use him as you see fit. Okay?" It was, and I hung up the phone.

"Am I being punished, Sergeant?"

"No, you're not. I'm going back to talk to Hawkins and Joe Thomas. I'm taking Detective Foote with me this time, to get a different perspective on both of them. I don't want for all three of us to go; that would be intimidating. So go give Mike a hand. He probably needs it."

He shook his head, stood, and reluctantly headed for the door. I sat for a minute, sipping my coffee, and thinking. "C'mon, Sarah. Let's go. Joe Thomas first, I think, then Mr. Hawkins."

CHAPTER 13

I DIDN'T CALL AHEAD. AS ALWAYS, I WANTED THE element of surprise on my side, and it was. I knew that Joe Thomas worked Saturdays, and so had Wednesdays off instead. Sure enough, he was home alone, Jasmine's parents being at the Heart Institute having Cletus's Coumadin levels checked.

Somehow, though, I got the impression that Joe wasn't surprised to see us. He opened the door, nodded, took a step back, and waved us in. We followed him into the living room where he dumped himself down into a huge easy chair, picked up the TV remote, and turned it off.

"So, what d'you want this time?" he asked. The tone was... wary.

I decided to go for the throat, "We checked your alibi, Mr. Thomas, for the night Jasmine was abducted. You don't have one. What you told me doesn't hold up. Yes, you bought new boots at Becky's but their copy of the receipt was timed at six-seventeen."

"Their register must be wrong," he said. "I know it was

after seven-thirty. It was; it was after seven-thirty, definitely."

"And you know that, how?"

"I... uh, well, I just know."

"It couldn't have been six-thirty? You're sure?"

"Yeah, I'm sure. I told ya. It was way later than that."

"Mr. Thomas," I said. "You're either mistaken, or you're lying. A mistake? Well, we all make them. But if you're lying—"

"I. Ain't. Lyin'."

"So, it was a mistake then?" I watched his eyes. They flickered. He looked away, lowered his chin.

You are *lying! What the hell...*

"I... I dunno. Maybe—"

"So, where were you?"

"SHIT!" he yelled. "I don't friggin' know. I was at Becky's until... hell, that's all I know."

I stared at him. He stared back, defiantly. I glanced sideways at Sarah. She looked at me, pursed her lips, then turned to look again at Thomas, as did I.

"Did you kill her, Joe?" I asked, quietly.

He jumped to his feet, "Holy shit! No, I friggin' didn't. We told you, Cletus an' me. We told you who done it. It was him, Hawkins! Go screw with him for Christ's sake, and leave me be... Okay, that's it. I've had enough of this bullshit. I want you outta here, right now. Go on. Get the hell up and get gone, and don't come back!"

And so we left him standing at the front door watching us leave. I had the feeling that it wouldn't be the last we saw of Mr. Joseph Thomas.

"So, Detective," I said to Sarah, as she turned the cruiser out of the Thomas driveway. "What do you think?"

"He sounds genuine enough, I suppose. Outraged, that's for sure. I kinda believed him."

"Kinda? How do you kinda believe someone? You either do or you don't."

"Okay," she said. "I believe him. He was righteously outraged."

"He was lying," I said. "All that blustering, it was just a cover up."

But was it?

There was just that one tell; he could have made a mistake in the timing. It was more than two weeks ago, and who keeps a log of their time?

RUSSELL HAWKINS WAS WORKING... if that's what you can call what he does. He didn't answer my knock at the front door, so we walked around the house and peered in the windows. We found him in a back room, hammering away at a computer keyboard. I knocked on the window and smiled to myself as the poor man almost came out of his seat, so surprised was he.

"Oh dear," he said when he opened the sliding glass door, "you startled me! Please, do come in. I'm working, but I could use a break. Fighting a war in space all by yourself is very tiring, as you can imagine. I always feel totally drained when I finally quit for the day. Now, Sergeant. What is it? What can I do for you? And who is this nice person you have with you? Where is the other nice man? I don't have too much time, but—"

I interrupted his flow. "This is Detective Foote. We just need a minute to clarify your whereabouts on the evening of the eleventh."

"Oh... you do? Hmmm. Well, please, sit down. I thought we went through all that. I was at a book signing at Barnes and Noble, at the mall. Did you not check?"

"Yes, Mr. Hawkins. We did. They said that the book signing was on the evening of the twelfth, the day after you claimed you were there."

"They did? Hmmm. Let me see..." He opened a drawer, brought out a date book, and started flipping through it. "That would have been Tuesday... Oh! It was Wednesday, Wednesday the twelfth! Hah, I could have sworn it was Tuesday. Must be getting old. My memory isn't what it was... not that it was ever that good, you understand—"

Again, I had to interrupt him, "Yes, yes, of course. So, if you weren't at B&N, where were you?"

"Where was I...?" He put a finger to his lips and closed his eyes, seemingly deep in thought. Then his eyes snapped open: "I was here. I must have been, because I can't think of anywhere else I might have been. So, here; I was here, at home."

"Is there anyone who can corroborate that?" I asked. "Was anyone here with you?"

"Oh no, no, no. I rarely have visitors. I don't have any friends... well, I do, but just one or two, and rarely do I talk to strangers. I did think about trying one of those online dating things, but I'm not a very outgoing person, you see. It's a lack of confidence, or so my ex-wife would say. But you know what? I don't believe it. I think I'm quite a confident person. Take my book signings, for instance. I—"

I turned and looked desperately at Sarah. She took the hint. "Mr. Hawkins? Please, sir," she said. "I'm afraid we're going to need a little more than that. What did you do that evening? Did you go out at all? If so, where, and did anyone see you?"

"No! No. I did not go out. I stayed in all day... wait. I did go out to the rim of the quarry and watch the children playing, but that was in the early afternoon, when I took a break from my writing. After that, I returned here, to the house and worked on until... oh, I don't know, five, five-thirty perhaps? Then I had dinner, pizza, I think it was, and a beer... Wait a minute. I ordered the pizza from Luigi's— they deliver, you know—so there you are, I did have a visitor after all!" he said, triumphantly.

"And what time would that have been?" Sarah asked.

"It must have been close to seven, I suppose. Maybe even a little later. I would have finished work, taken a shower, changed into something comfortable, and then made the call."

"Well," she said, "that's it then. It should be easy to check. I'm sure Luigi's keeps a record of their deliveries." She looked at me, quizzically. "Sergeant?"

"Yes," I said. "I think that should do it."

I rose to my feet, as did Foote. "Thank you, Mr. Hawkins. We'll be in touch."

"Yes, of course. Let me show you out."

I handed him one of my cards. "No need; we'll go out the way we came in. If you think of anything, please call me. That has my cell number on it."

We made our escape.

"Whew," Sarah said, as she engaged the starter. "That boy sure can talk. I think he's lonely."

"Yes," I said, sarcastically. "That's what he is, lonely, and no frigging wonder with a motor mouth like that. He can't help that, though. Anyway, other than his mouth, what do you think?"

"Nah," she said. "He didn't do it."

"Oh, and what makes you so sure?"

She shrugged, "I don't think he has it in him. It's just a feeling. That's all."

Just a feeling? Now, where have I heard that before? I wonder what he's doing today. Maybe I should give him a call... Nah. Later, perhaps.

She was right, of course. I didn't think he had it in him either, but that's what they said about Ted Bundy and John Wayne Gacy. And, boy, were they ever wrong about those two.

I heaved a huge sigh. Sarah turned to look at me, "What was that about?"

"Eh, nothing really. Just a little frustrated. Now I have two suspects, and neither one of them can properly account for their whereabouts, at least not yet. Let's head back to the office. I need to do some thinking; can you check Hawkins's alibi, such as it is? Hell, even if he did have pizza delivered at seven, or even seven-thirty, he could still have abducted Jasmine. And Joe Thomas, well..."

She nodded, and turned the cruiser toward Amnicola and home.

Sheesh, home? The station! I need to get a life. What time is it? I looked at my watch. It was almost noon. *Maybe I will call Harry. We could have lunch at the Boathouse.*

"Hey, Harry. It's me. You want to do lunch at the Boathouse? You're at the club. Oh, hell. It must be nice to be unemployed. You what? No, of course not; it's too far and too late. Tell August hello for me. See you tonight? Okay. Later."

Sarah looked sideways at me and grinned. "You could always take me instead."

"Indeed, I could. The Boathouse it is, then."

CHAPTER 14

Lunch at the Boathouse is always a good experience, and especially so on a glorious summer day. We managed to snag a table by the window overlooking the river. I ordered a Caesar Salad with iced tea, and so did Sarah. And then, for the first time in three days, during the day, I managed to relax for a few minutes. Unfortunately, my halcyon moment didn't last long.

Forty-five minutes later I was back at the office staring at my storyboard. It was pathetic, sadly lacking in detail and direction. Finally, I shook my head and gave up. I sat down at my desk, tapped the space bar on my computer keyboard, and entered my password.

I pulled up the Battery Heights area on Google Maps. It wasn't a huge area, maybe a little more than a half-mile across in any direction. I changed the view from streets to satellite, then to 3D. That brought up an aerial view of the area, with the quarry set slap bang in the middle. I enlarged the view until the scale was showing one hundred feet to the inch, and then I slowly began to search it, inch by inch.

It was a slow process. I'd been at it for almost an hour when I noticed something among the trees behind a small white house on the east side of Bonny Oaks Drive. It was the extreme edge of what I considered to be the area of interest; if I hadn't been looking for it, I would have missed it.

I enlarged the view slowly until I was seeing twenty feet to the inch at which point the quality of the image dropped off so much that the trees merged into one. I eased back a little. There it was. It wasn't much, just a small patch of brown amid the trees, maybe six feet by eight feet. The more I looked at it, the less certain I became as my eyes watered under the strain.

Screw this. I'll take a break and come back to it.

I went for coffee. I didn't want it, but it got me away from the screen. When I set the cup down beside the keyboard and looked again at the screen, the brown anomaly popped into focus.

It's part of a roof.

I enlarged it. It disappeared in a haze of fuzziness. I backed off.

Yes, that's what it is.

But as far as I could see, there was no access to it. It was perhaps sixty feet from the end of the back yard of the house. I stared at the tiny area for what must have been at least five minutes. I clicked on the house and Google supplied me with the address. I ran that through the system to find out who owned the property and...

Holy Shit. No frigging way.

The hair on the back of my neck prickling, I sat back in my chair, put my hands behind my neck, rolled away from the desk, and stared at the screen.

I. Do. Not. Believe it!

I picked up my phone and called John Tracy. He was out to lunch, but I told him to drop what he was doing and come pick me up. He readily agreed and said that he would leave right away. I nodded absently, unaware I was even doing it, and hung up.

I called Mike Willis.

"Hey, Mike. It's Kate Gazzara. How are you doing with the Honda?"

"It's slow going, Kate. It was completely flooded, fully immersed in the pond. We need to let it dry out naturally. If we use blowers, we could lose trace evidence. It will probably be tomorrow before we can make a start on it."

"Okay, that I can understand, but what the hell did you do with Tracy?"

"Oh, I kept him busy. He knows his drugs, I'll say that for him."

"Well," I said, "we'll talk again tomorrow then?"

"Sure, you can call me anytime... actually, how about I call you if I find anything? That way, neither of us will be wasting our time."

I agreed, hung up, and went back to my computer. The patch of brown—could it really be a roof?—was mesmerizing.

Where the hell is Tracy?

IT WAS JUST after two-thirty when Tracy pulled into the driveway of the Thomas home.

"Stay here," I told him. "I shouldn't be but a minute."

I got out of the car and pushed the doorbell. It was answered by Arlis Thomas.

"Oh, it's you. Come in. Have you found him?" Her eyes were wet from crying.

"I'm sorry, but no. Not yet. I have a quick question for you, though."

"Okay?"

"Is your husband home?"

"No. He went to Lowes for some screws."

I nodded. That suited me fine. "I understand you own a small property on Bonny Oaks, about a mile east. Is that correct?"

She nodded, slowly, "Ye-es. It's a rental, a little two-bedroom house, but it's vacant. Has been for more than a year. It needs a lot of work before we can rent it out. Why d'you ask?"

"You never mentioned it; neither one of you."

She shrugged, "I never even thought about it, and I'm sure Cletus didn't."

I nodded. It was reasonable. Why would they?

"I'd like to take a look at it; with your permission, of course. Do you have a key?"

"Yes, of course you can, but why?"

I hesitated for a moment, then said, "I'll be honest with you, Mrs. Thomas. I don't have a good reason. I'm just curious, that's all. Would you mind?" I looked at her, then said, "The key?"

She nodded. "I'll go get it." And she walked through to the kitchen. She was gone for several minutes, during which I could hear her searching through drawers. Finally, she returned, shaking her head.

"I can't find them. Let me call Cletus and see if he knows where they are."

She did. He didn't. He also wanted to know why I wanted into the house. I told her to tell him the truth. He said it was okay by him for me to enter the property, but not to break into the house, that he'd find us a key.

I didn't quite smile at that, but I was happy enough with his answer. It was the back yard I was interested in, not the house. At least not then. And now I had permission to enter the property, the yard at least. The house as well if I could find a way in without breaking anything. I thanked Arlis Thomas and returned to the cruiser.

IT WAS a little white frame house. It had an open porch at the front, facing Bonny Oaks, and a screened-in porch at the rear. The front door and windows were locked, but the screen door at the rear wasn't. Unfortunately, the back door itself was.

Tracy and I tried to look in the windows but all of them had blinds and we could see nothing.

Damn! Okay, now to the reason we're here.

I told Tracy to follow me and I headed away from the house across the yard. The grass hadn't been mowed in a couple of weeks. It was long but, thankfully, dry.

The perimeter of the property—maybe a hundred and twenty feet long by eighty wide—was delineated by a chain link fence. Just as I'd seen on Google Maps, it was surrounded by dense woodland. I walked the fence at the end of the property. It was overgrown, interwoven with long grass and weeds to the point where it was hard to tell it was even there.

Then I found it. It was maybe ten feet from the eastern edge of the property. The fence had been cut and the wire pushed back to make an opening. The grass beyond the fence had been trodden down. So had the grass inside the fence, but that had almost recovered, so it was harder to see.

I trod the grass down as I stepped through the gap. Tracy followed me through. The only thing on my mind right then was chiggers. Those little buggers love the long grass, and I'd been infested by them more than once. And itch? They could make life hell.

Anyway, the trail through the trees, if you could call it that, was almost completely overgrown and strewn with broken twigs and branches.

I made Tracy take the lead—what the hell good is rank if you don't take advantage of it?—and we pushed our way through the undergrowth... well, Tracy did. I followed in his footsteps, so to speak.

Finally, we emerged into a small clearing... and there it was, maybe thirty feet away. A derelict wooden barn, almost completely overgrown, walls leaning inward, rusty metal roof. There were two big wooden doors, one slightly overlapping the other. The sun filtered through the tree tops and glittered on what looked to be a brand-new lock and chain. I looked at the dirt in front of the doors. The half-circle scribed in the dirt told me that the door on the left had been opened many times; the dry dirt had been pushed aside, leaving a three-inch-high mound. And there were footprints. Everywhere. Dilapidated it might have been. But deserted? Not so much.

I felt a cold chill run down my spine. Somehow, I knew I was standing at the crime scene, the place where Jasmine Thomas had died.

"This is it," I said to Tracy. "This is what I was looking for."

He took a step forward. I grabbed his arm, "No! We can't, not yet."

As warm as it was, I shivered. More than anything in the world at that moment, I wanted to look inside that barn, but I knew I couldn't. Nor could I look around the outside, not only because most of it was so overgrown the barn was inaccessible, but because if it was a crime scene, I didn't want to disturb it.

I needed to call Mike Willis. The brand-new lock and chain on the barn door were tantalizing. *Reasonable suspicion?*

I thought so, and that provided me with probable cause to search the barn, even without a warrant. I already had permission to enter the house, but I wanted to cover my ass, do it right. I wanted a warrant to search both the barn and the house. Getting one wouldn't be a problem, I knew that, but I didn't want to leave the property.

I called Judge Henry Strange. I knew him well, and he was one of Harry's best friends. So long as I had my ducks in a row, I knew he would comply.

"Hello, Judge," I said when he answered his private cell phone. "This is Kate Gazzara. I hate to bother you, sir. I know how busy you must be, but I need a search warrant... quickly..." I closed my eyes and grimaced after I'd said it. I didn't know him quite that well.

There was a moment of silence, then: "Talk to me, Kate."

I explained what I needed and told him I had permission to enter the house but didn't know who owned the barn, and that I needed a warrant for the house and any outbuildings in its vicinity.

I could almost hear him thinking about it, "The house is no problem, you already have permission, but the barn. All you have is the lock and chain. That's a little thin on the PC, wouldn't you agree?"

"No, Judge. I have reasonable suspicion, based on the ownership of the rental, the hidden locale of the barn, and the brand-new lock and chain on a building that's nothing more than a falling down pile of lumber. That barn may well be my crime scene. The place where Jasmine Thomas was murdered."

He was quiet for a long moment, then I heard him sigh. "The house, the property, and the barn... all right, Kate. I'll draw it up now. Come and get it."

"Uh, if you don't mind, sir, I'll send Detective Tracy. I don't want to leave the property. You know how it is."

"I do. Send him on." And he disconnected without giving me a chance to thank him.

I sent Tracy on his way, then I called Mike Willis; it was just after three-fifteen.

"Hey, Mike," I said when he picked up. "I think I've found my crime scene. I need you to bring a team to a rental property on Bonny Oaks, a two-bedroom house with an old barn out back. The house is locked up tight, but Tracy is on his way to pick up a warrant. Can you handle it?"

He could.

"You're going to need bolt cutters, big ones. Park in the driveway and come through the yard all the way to the... no, wait. I'll meet you out front."

I gave him the address, "It's urgent, Mike. How long will you be? Thirty minutes? Twenty would be a whole lot better. Okay. I'll be out front waiting for you." I went to the front porch of the house and sat down on the steps to wait.

True to his word, Willis arrived twenty minutes later. "So, what do we have?" he asked, as he exited his vehicle. He was alone.

"Are you it?" I asked, hoping to hell he wasn't.

"Nooo," he said. "I'm just the spearhead. The rest of the team will be here momentarily. Tell me, Kate. What's going on?"

"I need this house processed." I turned and looked at it; so did he. "But not yet. What I'm most interested in is the old barn back there among the trees. We haven't touched anything; hell, we didn't even approach it. There are footprints, and there's a steel lock and chain on the door that probably have prints on them." I took a breath. He watched me intently. "The barn, Mike. I think that's where she was killed."

"What makes you think that?" he asked.

"Nothing specific. It's just a feeling. Instinct, intuition, whatever."

He nodded, walked a few steps down the side of the house, and stared out at the yard and the trees beyond. Then he came back and opened the rear doors of his vehicle.

"Best to suit up out here, I think. Help yourself."

I donned Tyvek coveralls and latex gloves; the booties I'd carry with me to the barn and put them on there. The hair cover...

Damn, I hate those things.

I decided to carry that too.

I was just about ready when the rest of Mike's CSI team arrived. He had a quick word with them, grabbed a huge set of bolt cutters from a tool box in the back of the vehicle, and we headed for the barn.

We broke through the trees into the small clearing and Willis stopped and held up his arm; I almost ran right into him.

For several minutes he stood silently, surveying the area, then he nodded and said, "This way."

He led us to the right, around the perimeter of the clearing—if such a small area can even have a perimeter. It was no more than a few yards before we were at the front wall.

"Booties, please," he said.

I put them on and followed him, taking care to disturb the dry, dusty ground as little as possible.

He stood in front of the two doors, then crouched down with the bolt cutters across his knees and examined the lock and chain without touching them. Then he stood, took the tool in both hands, looked at me, and said, "Kate? If you would." He nodded at the lock and chain. "I don't want them to fall in the dirt."

I took hold of the chain. He set the cutters on the shackle of the lock and pressed. It was a monster of a lock, the shackle made of hardened steel at least three-eighths of an inch thick. It took m'man Mike a couple of tries, then suddenly the shackle gave with a crack that rivaled a pistol shot, and the assembly dropped loose in my hand.

Willis took an evidence baggie from the pack he had slung over his shoulder and opened it. I dropped the lock and chain into it, and he sealed and signed it. I counter-signed, and handed it off to one of the techs.

The two doors were each about six feet wide and seven feet high; the wood had weathered to a dirty gray. They'd seen better days, and sagged until both touched the floor. The right-hand door, deeply embedded in the dirt, looked as if it hadn't been opened in years. Not so the one on the left; as I'd noticed earlier, it had been dragged through the dirt many times.

Willis handed me the cutters, grabbed the door with both hands, and pulled. It gave a couple of inches, the top moving almost a foot. And that's how he did it. Pull after pull, several inches at a time, until he had a gap big enough for us to slide through.

It was dark inside, and hot, and dry. The temperature outside the barn was in the low nineties; inside, it had to be twenty degrees hotter / higher.

I had a tiny flashlight on my keychain. Unfortunately, there was no way for me to get at it through the protective coveralls.

I stood for a minute, my eyes slowly adjusting to the low light. Then a great beam shone across the interior; Mike was holding one of those big rechargeable flashlights with an adjustable beam.

"Kate, we need to get some lights in here, but we can't do that until my guys have processed the approaches." His "guys" were one male and three female techs.

It took them another hour to clear the approaches to the barn. Then I had to wait impatiently for another fifteen minutes while they brought in three large portable lights and a generator.

Then, finally, "I don't suppose you'd like to stay outside for a few minutes, would you, Kate?"

"As the saying goes, Mike: not only no, but hell no. Let's get on with it, for God's sake." And we did.

The techs set up the lights to illuminate the entire interior. Mike and I stood silently by as they did so. Slowly, one light at time, all was revealed.

The barn, if it could have been called that, must at one time have been a stable or cow shed. There were three stalls, now dilapidated almost beyond recognition, along the right side. A pile of rotting wood boards was stacked against the left side. The rest of the space, an open area maybe twenty feet by thirty feet, stretched the entire length of the structure. Throughout the structure was a dirt floor, dry and dusty. A small propane lantern, bright red and obviously quite new, stood on the stack of boards.

But what caught my eye was the chair at the far end, lying on its side in the center of the open space. I shuddered. I looked at Tracy, now returned from his trip. His face was a mask, his features drawn tight; he nodded at me. Mike had that enigmatic half-smile on his face. What he was thinking, I had no idea.

"Hmmm. Interesting," he said, eventually. "I think we might have something here. See the pieces of duct tape on the back of the chair?"

I hadn't, but I did then, and I felt my heart begin to race.

"Let's go take a look," Mike said. "I'll go first; you follow, carefully. Try to step in my footsteps and when I tell you stop, you stop, yes?"

We nodded, and followed Mike in single file as he made his way slowly and carefully across the floor. I can't imagine what the three of us must have looked like, dressed in whites from head to toe, creeping along in unison like the Three Stooges in a haunted house.

It sounds hilarious, I know. It wasn't.

Suddenly, Mike held up his hand: "Stop." And bitch-slap me if Tracy didn't bang right into my back.

"Dammit, John. For God's sake, give me a little space, will you?"

"Yeah, Boss, sorry, I wasn't—"

"I know you weren't," I said, irritated. "But you'd better."

"Hey, you two." Mike turned. "Simmer down. This ain't a friggin' bar. Stay right where you are. I want to look at the area around the chair."

He took two more steps forward, leaving me feeling like a scolded child.

Damn you, Tracy.

Mike reached the chair, stooped down, and stared intently at it, and the dirt floor under and around it. He must have stayed like that for five minutes or more before poking a forefinger into the dust. He put his finger to his nose and breathed deeply. He nodded to himself, then stood and turned around.

"Okay," he said, crisply. "Outside, please, both of you, and be careful where you put your feet."

So we turned and trooped back across the open space and out the door.

Once safely outside, I turned to Mike and said, "You found something. What?"

"I'm not entirely sure. Urine, I think. It's dried out, but there's a slight discoloration in the dirt where the chair stood. It does have an odor, but not much. I don't know if we can get enough material to extract DNA, but we'll try."

I nodded, and he continued. "The tape. It looks like it's been used as a restraint. I can see what appears to be blood on it. Did you see the lamp?"

"Yes, of course."

"Did you see what was beside it on the plank?"

"No... what?"

"Again, I'm not sure. Some sort of flimsy fabric, balled up; could be underwear."

Her bra and panties.

"So, this is it, then?" I asked. "This is the crime scene?"

He shrugged. "We'll see. It's going to take most of the rest of the day and night to process the building. I can't have you here. You need to leave."

It was said in a friendly manner, but there was no doubt he meant what he said, so I nodded.

"Of course, but..."

"But what?" he asked.

"The house. If this is what we think it is, then I think maybe we should take a look at it. We have enough probable cause to break in."

"Ummm..." He looked over his shoulder at the activity inside the barn, then turned back and said, "Give me a minute. I don't want you doing that without me."

He went back inside the barn and spoke to one of the techs, who nodded vigorously. Then Mike left him and came back to us.

"Let's do it," he said. "We'll go into the house, take a quick look around, see what we can see, then out of there. Agreed?"

"Agreed."

We returned to the small white house, where we waited while Mike went to his vehicle to "get some tools." We entered the screened-in porch through the unlocked door. The door into the house took no more than a couple of minutes to open; the tools Mike had fetched were lock picks.

"Whew," he said, as he pushed the door open. "It's hot as hell in here."

He flipped the light switch. The kitchen light came on.

"Hmmm. The power's on," he said. "The AC must be turned off. Holy crap!" He grabbed his nose. "What's that stink? The place smells like a sewer, oh, m'God."

And it did: the air inside the house was musty, but beyond that, there was an overpowering smell of... well, something unmentionable.

We made our way through the house, from room to room. We found the source of the stench. The commode in the bathroom off the hall had been used, several times by the look of it, and hadn't been flushed. Mike turned the water faucet: nothing.

"The water's turned off," he said, stating the obvious.

The rest of the rooms, with one exception, were completely empty. In one of the bedrooms were two pieces of furniture: a king-size bed and a nightstand. The bed was unmade, the covers rumpled, turned back. The bottom sheet was stained and I could see several long brown hairs on the pillows. Two glasses, one half full of some sort of clear liquid, were on the nightstand beside the bed.

Willis stepped into the room, lifted the glass to his nose, sniffed, and then replaced it.

"Sprite, I think. Flat. Several days old, at least."

He walked to the far side of the bed and lifted the covers.

He slowly shook his head. "This has seen a lot of action." He looked at me. "Stains, lots of them."

"Semen?"

"Yeah, looks like it."

"DNA, then?"

"Yeah, for sure. When the guys get finished in the barn, I'll have 'em start in here..." he looked around. "We're talking several days' work, at least. Prints? I can have Margo run them as we find them. The rest? We won't know much until the work is complete. For now, I suggest you go home and get some rest. I'll call if I find anything significant. If not, we'll talk tomorrow, at the office."

I nodded, and the three of us left the house. Mike closed and relocked the door behind him.

"I'll have this place sealed until we can get to it. I'll talk to you tomorrow, Kate. See you, John." And then he walked off through the long grass, back toward the barn.

I sighed, shook my head, frustrated. I never did have a whole lot of patience; being shut out and told to wait for, hell, who knew how long, didn't help at all. I felt totally useless, and there was nothing I could do about it, not until I had some facts.

Damn it!

I shook off my frustration, glanced at my watch—it was almost six.

Wow! It's that late? Sheesh.

And suddenly I realized I was hungry. I'd eaten nothing but a bagel for breakfast and a salad for lunch. *Damn, a bowl of lettuce ain't gonna get it. I need some meat and taters.*

"Take me back to my car, John. I'm going to have an early night." Well, that was my intention. But, as the saying goes, the road to hell...

CHAPTER 15

John Tracy dropped me at my car. I pushed the starter and called Harry.

"Hey," I said when he picked up. "I'm hungry. Would you like to take me to dinner?"

"Sure. Where would you like to go?"

"You name it. Anything will do so long as they serve meat... and wine."

"We can do that. You coming here or what?"

"No. I need to go home. Pick me up in an hour, say seven-thirty?"

"You got it."

Any other night I would have gone to Harry's, but that night, I needed to be at home, to think.

True to his word, an hour later almost to the minute, my doorbell rang. Then I heard Harry's key in the lock. And, wouldn't you know it. I wasn't ready.

Not that I was getting dressed for a ball, just jeans and a blouse, but the minute I'd gotten home I had poured myself a large glass of red, and dumped myself down on the sofa.

And then poured myself another one. And then I glanced at the clock and almost flipped out: it was already ten after seven and I hadn't even showered. I knew that Harry would be on time; the OCD SOB always was. There were times when his punctuality was almost more than I could handle, that and his catting... Oh no. We won't go there.

"Hey," he said, sliding onto a stool at the breakfast bar. "You're a little out of whack. What's up?"

"It's been a long day. That's all," I replied, not wanting to go into details.

Hah, fat chance of that.

But he nodded and didn't push it. "I've booked a table at Ruth's Chris. That work for you?"

Hell yes, it worked for me.

"Great. Just let me clean up and we'll go."

We ordered crab cakes for the appetizer. I ordered a twelve-ounce fillet with a blue cheese crust and a "one pounder" baked potato, loaded. Harry had the fresh lobster with fries. He ordered a bottle of Pinot Noir for me and a glass of Chardonnay for himself.

By the time the entrée was served, it was almost nine o'clock. But who was counting? I certainly wasn't. I was totally relaxed. I'd just poured my second glass of Pinot and taken a second bite of one of the best steaks I'd ever eaten when—you guessed it—my cell phone buzzed on the table beside my plate. I picked it up and checked the number. I didn't recognize it, and I almost didn't answer the call, but then... something told me I should. So I did.

"Sergeant Gazzara?"

"Uh, yes?"

"Ah, good, Sergeant. I'm glad I was able to get you.

This is Nurse Gains at Erlanger Emergency. I have a Mr. Russell Hawkins here. He was brought in with gunshot wounds just over an hour ago. He's been quite agitated, and asking for you. He says he needs to talk to you."

Holy crap!

I looked at Harry, not knowing what to say to the nurse. He gazed back at me, quizzically.

"His wounds; are they life-threatening?" I asked.

"No, not at the moment, but he was shot in both knees and he's lost a lot of blood. He's heavily sedated and rambling: he's about to go into surgery. He'll be in there for a while, I'm sure."

"Okay, thank you, Nurse. Listen, I need to send someone over to keep an eye on things until I get there. D'you have any idea what time he'll get out of surgery?"

"No, ma'am, I don't. His wounds are severe, and he's going to need extensive surgery. My best guess would be at least five hours."

Damn, there goes my beauty sleep.

"Okay, I understand. I'll have Detective Tracy there as soon as I can. Can he ask for you?"

"He certainly can. He may not get me, however, so it's best he goes to the front desk. I'll let them know he's coming."

"Fine. I'll be there as soon as I can."

The hell I will.

I thanked her and disconnected, sat for a moment staring at the screen, then looked at Harry, "Excuse me, one more minute, okay?"

He nodded, that wicked little smirk on his lips. Yes, he

knew. He'd been through it all himself, a thousand times; we both had.

I hit the speed dial, put the phone to my ear and waited, and waited, until finally I got Tracy's voicemail...

Damn it all to hell.

"Tracy," I growled. "By God you'd better call me back in the next ten minutes or your ass will be grass. Ten. Minutes. Got it?"

Not thirty seconds later, my phone buzzed.

"Hey," Tracy said. "It's me. What's the panic?"

That did it. "Panic? There's no damn panic. But when I call you, I expect you to answer, goddammit. You don't get to screen your calls when you're working with me. Now get your ass over to Erlanger. Hawkins has been shot. He's getting prepped right now for surgery. I have no idea what the hell happened. I want you to watch over him until I get there. Don't take any crap from anyone. We don't know who did it, or if they'll try to finish the job. I'll get there whenever I can. Got that?"

"Yeah, I got it. Where are you now?"

"That's none of your damn business. Just get your ass over there. Now!" And I hung up on him. I stared down at my steak, and I swear it stared right back up at me.

Next, I called Mike Willis to ask if they were processing the Hawkins residence. I didn't need to ask; I knew they were. The first responding officer would have taken care of that. But I had to make sure. Mike was already on site.

"Hey, I heard what happened to Hawkins. D'you need me?" I asked.

"Nah! There's nothing you can do here, Kate. I have it in hand. I'll see you tomorrow, okay?"

"Okay. See you then." I disconnected, sat back in my chair, threw back my head, and stared, unseeing, up at the ceiling.

"I take it you have a problem," Harry said, quietly.

"Yes, I have a problem, and it's all your damn fault. If you hadn't gone and quit..." I glared at him across the table, and then I softened.

"Oh, hell, Harry. Of course it's not your fault. It's not your fault that I'm stuck with an idiot for a partner. It's not his fault either. That he's an idiot, I mean.

"Anyway, as you probably heard, one of my suspects has been shot, both knees. I'll need to get over there..." I looked at my watch, "but not until later, one o'clock, or two. Idiot Tracy is on his way over there now, and Hawkins won't be out of surgery for a while, and even if he was, I'm not passing on this steak. I'm going to eat it, enjoy it, then drink a gallon of coffee to sober up before I head on over there... You want to come with me?"

What a stupid question. Of course he doesn't.

He just smiled at me and shook his head.

Oh well. It was worth a shot.

Harry dropped me off at my apartment around ten-thirty with instructions for me to call him whenever.

Me? I took a long, hot shower, then set the alarm on my phone for one in the morning. All tasks completed, I collapsed, naked, on top of the bed and was out like a light...

...only to startle awake, in what seemed like mere minutes, to the sound of the alarm; I thought the world was ending.

Oh, m'God, that was a bad idea, sleeping, I thought groggily, as I all but fell off the bed.

I staggered to my closet, hopped around like a circus clown trying to get into a clean pair of panties... hah, you think that's funny, you should have seen the antics when it came time for the jeans.

I wonder if Harry meant it when he offered me a job... Nah, I can't go there.

CHAPTER 16

IT WAS AFTER TWO IN THE MORNING WHEN I walked through the doors of the Emergency Unit at Erlanger Hospital. I made myself known at the front desk and they told me where to go... No, not like that. They gave me Hawkins's room number and explained to me how to get there. Tracy was seated outside the door with an iPad on his knees.

They'd just wheeled Hawkins in and were in the process of making him comfortable, if that was even possible, but he was still out of it. I was informed that it would be at least a couple of hours before he would be able to talk.

Oh, hell, I thought. *What a way to spend a night.*

I hate hospitals with a passion. There are no good experiences to be had in any ward of any hospital, not even a maternity unit. And Erlanger... well, let me put it this way... if I'd been shot, there's no place on Earth I'd rather be. As a visitor, any other place on Earth is where I'd rather be.

And there I was, faced with at least a couple of hours in

a hospital waiting room, in the dead of night, with only Idiot Tracy for company. *Oh, m'God!*

But it was actually worse than that. Two hours, they'd said, but it was almost seven in the morning before they finally let me in to see him.

He looked like hell. There was a dressing on his forehead, above his left eye, and his face was pale, almost bloodless. But he was breathing evenly, and his vital signs were running smoothly across that hypnotic monitor all hospital rooms are equipped with. His pulse was steady; his blood pressure looked good to me, but what do I know.

"Hey," I quietly said, lightly touching his shoulder.

His eyes opened immediately. "Hello, Sergeant Gazzara," he said, weakly. "I hope you feel better than I do."

It was a small attempt at humor, and that was something, but the fire had gone from his eyes. He was a shadow, a pathetic little man, sore and hurting, in more ways than just from the shots to his knees. I couldn't help but feel sorry for him.

"Do you feel like talking?" I asked.

He nodded.

"Can you tell me what happened?"

Again, he nodded, "There's not much to tell. It happened so quickly; two or three minutes is all. It was just after eight o'clock. I know because I'd just turned on Fox news, I like to watch Tucker Carlson..." For a moment, I thought he was back on form and about to launch into a diatribe about his viewing habits, but he didn't.

"Anyway," he continued, weakly. "I thought I heard someone at the back door. I went to see who was there, but there was no one. I was just closing the door when it slammed open, knocking me backward, and a man dressed all in black barged in..." He paused, took a breath; he was obviously in pain. I said nothing, waited for him to continue.

"He grabbed me by my shirt, pushed me all the way into the living room and down onto the sofa. Then he called me some really nasty names and accused me of killing Jasmine. I told him I didn't, but either he didn't care or didn't hear. He took a pistol from his belt and waved it in my face. He said he was going to make me pay for it. Then he hit me in the head with the gun and..."

"Did you recognize him?" I asked.

He shook his head, "No, he was wearing one of those ski mask things, a really scary one."

"How about his voice? Did you recognize that?"

He thought about it for a minute, then shook his head, "No, it sounded like he had something in his mouth."

"So, there's nothing you remember about him, nothing you can tell me that might help me find him?"

"No, I don't think so. I don't even remember him shooting me. I do remember seeing him crawling around on his knees, and even hurting as much as I was, I couldn't help wondering why."

I thought I knew why, but I didn't mention it to Hawkins. Instead, I told him to get some rest, and that I would talk to him again soon. Then I left. I needed to talk to Mike Willis.

I FOUND Mike in his office. He looked tired, and so he should. To my knowledge, the man had been going at it forty-eight hours straight.

He looked up when I knocked on his door. He gestured for me to enter, and I did. I dropped into the seat in front of his desk. I was just about done in myself.

"So," I said. "Long night?"

He nodded and stretched. "Yep. You know it. How about you?"

"Weird. Totally weird."

"I bet. How's Harry?"

"He's good. Enjoying life."

"No change, then?" He grinned.

"No, no change. So," I said, changing the subject. "What do you have for me?"

"I think I might have your man for you."

"You do?" I straightened up in the chair. "Who? Who is it?"

He sat back in his chair, smiling. "We found a nine-millimeter casing at the Hawkins house. It was down among the cushions in the sofa."

So, I was right. I figured he was looking for something.

"He must have picked up the other one. Anyway," he said, as he handed the paper evidence baggie across the desk. "I'll need you to sign for that. There's an absolutely beautiful thumb print on it. He must have made it when he loaded the mag. There's another partial print on the chain we cut off the barn doors. It belongs to the same person. The chain to the quarry gate, the old one? We never found it. The killer must have taken it away with him."

I took the bag and held it up so I could see the casing

through the transparent window. Then I nodded, grabbed a pen from his desktop, and added my name to the list on the baggie.

"And we ran Jasmine Thomas's phone records," he continued. "She received several calls the night she was abducted... from the same guy. The stains on the bedding are semen. One of the hairs has its follicle attached. The urine in the barn is human. So DNA? I think so, but it's going to take a while, maybe three or four weeks."

He stared at me, smiling.

He's frigging teasing me.

"Oh, come on, Mike. Out with it. Who the hell is it?"

He leaned forward, still smiling; without saying a word, he pushed a ten card across the desk. I picked it up, looked at the name, then looked at Mike, my eyes wide in question.

"No shit?" I wasn't all that surprised.

"No shit."

"Thank you, my friend. I owe you one." I stood and handed the card to him.

"Go get him, Kate."

I nodded, and left him sitting there, smiling.

CHAPTER 17

WHEN I LEFT MIKE'S OFFICE, I WASN'T QUITE SURE what to do next. Sure, I had my man. But I'd never been in this situation before. It had always been Harry, with me as backup. So, I decided to take a minute to think. My man wasn't going anywhere and I wanted to savor the moment. This was, after all, my first. There never would be another one.

I looked around the room, knowing that no one knew what I knew, and it felt good. Very good.

I called Harry.

"Guess what?" I asked when he answered.

"You know who done it," he answered promptly.

"How the hell did you know that?" I asked, more than a little pissed off.

"Why else would you call me?"

"Maybe I wanted to tell you how much I love you, you frigging ass."

"I already know that, and I love you too, sweetheart. Now go get him, and enjoy the moment. You're going to love it. You have no idea how much. Don't call me; you can tell me all about it tonight, over a very expensive bottle of champagne." And he hung up, leaving me staring at the phone.

You frigging ass, Harry Starke.

I called Chief Johnston.

"Hello, Kate," he said, before I could say anything. "You have good news for me, I hope? The media, and the mayor, are all over my ass about this 'Girl in the Pipe' thing. Do you have a solution yet?"

"I do—"

"When will you make the arrest?"

"Today, if—"

"See that you do. Is there anything else? I'm extremely busy."

"Well, since you ask—"

"Good, good. Let me know how it goes. We'll talk to the press together. That is, I'll talk, you'll listen, capisce?" And he hung up on me.

Damn! No wonder Harry hates the man. Yes, I frigging capisce. You'll take the credit while I stand there and look stupid.

Sarah Foote had the day off. Something to do with her mother, she'd said, but I hadn't paid much attention. That wasn't like me, but what the hell, I had a lot on my mind.

Idiot Tracy, however, was at his desk.

"Hey, John. I need you."

He came over and sat down, "Yeah? What d'ya need?"

Inwardly, I rolled my eyes. "We have a call to make—"

"So make it," he said, picking up my phone and handing it to me.

"No, John. Not a phone call. We have to go visiting, but first I need you to go and pick up a warrant from Judge Strange. When you get back, call me and I'll meet you in the parking lot. We'll go together."

I called Henry Strange and told him what I needed. Again, the man asked for probable cause—which I now had, aplenty—and he agreed to issue the warrant. Which was good, because Tracy had already left for the courthouse.

WE ARRIVED at the house on Wickman Lane at just after five that afternoon. We could see that Joe's Silverado was parked at the side of the house next to the Thomases' Cadillac. The truck had one of those crossover toolboxes mounted behind the cab.

I parked out front, walked the few feet to the front door, and thumbed the doorbell. The door opened almost immediately.

"Hello, Mr. Thomas. We need to talk to Joe. Is he in?"

"Yeah, he's in the living room. Why d'you wanna talk to him?"

"I have some questions I need to ask him. Can we use your office?"

"Yeah, I suppose."

"Thank you. Mrs. Thomas not home?"

"Nah. She's gone to the grocery store."

I nodded.

"Hey, Joe," Cletus said, as we followed him into the living room. "The p'lice have more questions for you. What would they want with you?"

Joe Thomas rose from the sofa where he'd been watching television and leveled a hard gaze at me. "I dunno. What *do* you want?"

"In private," I said, "if you don't mind, sir."

"Huh? What the hell?"

"Please, Mr. Thomas."

Reluctantly, he made his way to Cletus's office and sat down behind the desk table. I closed the door, leaving Cletus outside, then I turned on my recorder and placed it on the table in front of Joe.

"So what the hell d'you want now?" he asked angrily, staring down at the tiny machine.

"For the purposes of this interview, and to make sure nothing is misinterpreted, I'll be recording everything that's said," I warned him. "Do you understand, Mr. Thomas?"

He said he did, and for the record, I stated the date and time, the names of those present, and the purpose of the interview. Then I dove right in.

"We checked your phone records. You called Jasmine at six-thirty-two and talked for almost two minutes. What was that about? Did you arrange to meet her?"

He stared at me; the color had drained from his face.

"I didn't talk to her. I got her voicemail."

"Did you leave a message?"

He hesitated, then said, "No."

"Why not? Why did you call her at all?"

"I told you, we were friends. We talked, sometimes. When she didn't answer, I just hung up."

"I don't believe you, Joe."

He shrugged, looked away, then said, "So what. It's the truth."

I changed the subject. "Tell me about Russell Hawkins."

He screwed up his eyes, frowned, then asked, "What about him?"

"It was you, wasn't it? You beat him up then shot him in the knees."

"You're friggin' crazy. You can't prove that shit."

"Hawkins doesn't know who attacked him," I said. "Whoever it was, he was wearing a mask. *You* were wearing a mask."

He just stared at me, saying nothing.

"The 911 call came from Hawkins's cell phone, but we know he didn't make that call, because he told us he didn't. You made that call, didn't you, Joe?"

Again, he said nothing, a slight smirk on his lips.

"It was you, wasn't it Joe? You attacked Hawkins and you used his cell phone to call 911."

"You know what, Sergeant," he said. "You're so full o' shit. The truth is, you don't have a thing. No proof, no gun, no nothin', an' he don't know who shot him—"

"Ah, but that's where you're wrong," I said. "I have all the proof I need. I have this."

I reached into my jacket pocket for the paper evidence bag and held it up for him to see. The nine-millimeter shell casing glinted through the transparent plastic window.

"Yeah, so? That don't prove nothin'"

"We found it between the cushions of Hawkins's sofa. You found one casing, but not this one. You must not have seen where it landed."

He frowned, his eyes narrowed, his face pale, "So what?

Even I know a casing don't prove nothin' without the gun. Which you don't have, right?"

"That's right, we don't."

His confidence returned, along with his smirk.

"So, get the hell gone. Come back when you have some proof. I didn't do nothin' wrong."

"Actually," I said, smiling, waving the envelope in his face, "this is all I need."

"But you said—"

"No, I didn't. You did. You're right. I don't have the gun, but I don't need it. What I have is a perfect thumb print on this casing. It's yours, and you made it when you pushed the shell into the mag. Gotcha, Joe."

I smiled at him as I unhooked the cuffs from my belt.

"Joseph Thomas, I'm arresting you for the attempted murder of Russell Hawkins."

"Hey. Whoa. Attempted murder?"

"Oh yes. You used a deadly weapon. You shot him in the legs and you left him. He could have bled out. He still might die from some sort of infection," I said, as I snapped on the second cuff.

"Why did you do it, Joe?"

I thought for a minute that he wasn't going to answer, but he did.

"Yeah, I did. I shot him," he said defiantly. "The slimy little prick killed Jasmine. An' I know you're not gonna get him for that, that's for sure. So I made sure he got what was comin' to him. I put him on sticks for the rest of his life, I hope, and the on'y reason I didn't kill him was because I didn't want to spend the rest of my life in prison."

I nodded, "Ah, but you might. Attempted murder

carries a penalty of seven years to life. You may not have intended to kill him, and you did call 911, but the minute you left him alone the charge changed from assault with a deadly weapon to attempted murder. But whatever, I'll let the DA sort that out. Now, to continue. Sit down."

He sat, and so did we.

"Before we go any further, Joe, I need to read you your righ—"

"Screw m'rights," he growled. "I just told you I did it."

"You sure, Joe? I'm not done yet."

"Yeah? Well just get the hell on with it."

"You and I both know that Hawkins didn't kill Jasmine. You did. I know you killed her, Joe," I said, gently.

"*What?* Me? I killed her? You're crazy!"

"I'm not crazy, Joe, but I think you might be. I know you killed her, and I think the attack on Russell Hawkins was your attempt to divert attention away from you."

"No! No! *No!*"

"Yes, Joe. You did, so why don't you make it easy on yourself. Tell me what happened."

"That's crazy! Why would I do that?"

"I think you were abusing her sexually. And I think she'd had enough. That's why, Joe."

"That ain't true. I didn't kill her."

"Oh, I think it is, and I think you did, and I have proof. You really didn't need to cripple Hawkins. That was your plan, wasn't it, Joe. You were sweating. You thought I was onto you, so you wanted me to think that you thought it was him, therefore you couldn't have done it. But you were right. I was onto you. In fact, I already had you. I can place you at one crime scene, the barn where you killed her, and I can place both you and Jasmine in the rental on Bonny Oaks. I had enough to charge you right there but I figured I needed more. I still needed to be able to place you at the dump site."

I watched him. He stared stoically back at me.

"No comment, Joe? Don't you want to know what I know?"

He didn't answer, just glared straight at me.

"You were careful, Joe, I'll give you that, but I *can* place you at that barn. We found a matching print on that shiny new lock and chain you put on the barn doors."

"That don't prove nothin'!"

"True, Joe. It really doesn't prove a whole lot; only that you were there. It's circumstantial at best. But you know what, Joe? It does give me probable cause to search your room and your truck."

"You can't do that; not without a warrant."

"Detective Tracy," I said, without taking my eyes off my victim.

Tracy took the folded warrant from his pocket and waved it in Thomas's face. "And here it is," he said, rising from his seat. "You want me to go take a look, Boss?"

"I do. Do you have a key to that tool box on your truck, Mr. Thomas? It doesn't matter if you don't. I have bolt cutters in my car."

"My ass pocket," he said, getting up and turning his ass to Tracy. "You won't find nothin'. Ain't nothin' there to find."

"If that's true," I said, "you've got nothing to worry about. Go take a look, Detective. Take Cletus with you. I wouldn't want our friend here to claim we'd planted evidence. We'll wait here for you. Oh, and don't let Cletus know what you're looking for, or why."

Tracy was gone for no more than a few minutes, then he returned and closed the door behind him; he was grinning widely.

"Find anything?" I asked.

He held up a length of rusty chain in his latex gloved hand and let it dangle in front of Joe Thomas's face. Actually, it was two pieces of chain held together at the ends by a large padlock.

"Okay," Thomas said. "You got a piece o' chain, so what?"

"Let's think about that for a minute, Joe," I said, leaning back in my chair, smiling at him, "and see where it takes us. That lock is numbered, right Detective?"

He examined it. "Yeah, it's numbered."

"I thought so. It's city property, so it was inventoried and there'll be a record of when it was issued and where it was located. Where do you think it was located, Joe?"

I was thoroughly enjoying myself. Now I knew how Harry had felt during these situations. It was *fun!*

Again, Joe played Br'er Rabbit and said nothing.

"I'll tell you where I think you got it, shall I? You cut it off the gate blocking the access road into the quarry, and you replaced it with a brand-new one, right? No comment, Joe? I don't blame you. You were wearing gloves then, weren't you? That new chain is clean. This one? It's probably clean too, but it doesn't matter because either way—if there are prints on it or not—though I'm betting there are, since we found it in your truck. Just the fact that you have it, and that we can prove where you got it, is enough to...

shall we say, hang you. But they don't do that anymore, do they, Joe?"

No answer, so I said, "Talk to me, Joe. Tell me what happened."

Again, he just glared at me and said nothing.

"Okay," I said. "I think I know exactly how it went. You were having sex with Jasmine. For how long I don't know, but I do know you were."

He was shaking his head, his face white, "That's not... I wasn't... I didn't never. I wouldn't—"

"Yes, you were, and I have proof. You used to take her to the rental, didn't you? You had sex with her there. I have her DNA and yours, both were found among the sheets on the bed."

I didn't know that for sure, but Harry always liked to play that game, and it worked for him so why not me?

I watched his eyes; he'd swallowed my bluff. "How long had it been going on, Joe? Did she finally tell you it was over, that if you didn't leave her alone she'd go to the police? That's the trouble with minors; they have a habit of growing up. Is that what happened, Joe. It is, isn't it? And you decided you couldn't have that, so you killed her."

The door burst open. "Joe," Cletus said, quietly. "Look at me, Joe. Please tell me what she's sayin' ain't true."

Shit, he must have been outside the door listening.

Joe said nothing.

"Goddammit, you're my brother," Cletus whispered. "She was your niece." He stared at Joe, unbelieving, slowly shaking his head. "Tell me you didn't do it."

Joe Thomas looked around wildly, then a great calm imbued his very being. "I loved her," he said, softly and reverently. "I always loved her. She, she loved me too. I know she did, because... Then... I dunno; she changed, she started avoidin' me. Then she told me we had to stop, that I was, that I was a... friggin' pedophile! And that she was gonna go to the police an' tell 'em! I couldn't allow that, I had to stop her. I, I, she... I had to talk to her. I called her, that night. I begged her to meet me. She didn't want to, but she did. I picked her up outside The Gap at Hamilton Place. We talked. I tried to make her see, but..." he shrugged, shook his head, looked up at Cletus, then continued. "I took her to the rental. It was almost dark. I drove down the side of the house, so's no one could see, then I smacked her upside o' the head and carried her to the barn... That's it... I'm sorry, Cletus. I loved her so much—"

"But she wasn't dead, was she, Joe?" I asked.

He shook his head.

"So, you tied her up," I continued, "and you had sex with her for five days and then you—"

"You sick bastard!" Cletus yelled, reaching behind him.

Before either Tracy or I could move, Cletus pulled a gun from his belt and pointed it first at his brother, then at Tracy, then at me.

"Don't none o' ya move. You do, an' I'll kill ya. I'll kill y'all. I swear it."

He directed his attention, and the gun, back to his brother. "Why, Joe? Why'd you kill her? You didn't have to. She wouldn'a told no one. You knew her. She wouldn'a done that, she wouldn't."

They stared at each other, Joe's eyes flicking between his brother's face and the unwavering gun in Cletus's hand.

Oh... I don't like where this is going.

I glanced at Tracy. He was wound tight, head cocked, ready to make his move. I caught his eye, shook my head just slightly. He nodded, relaxed a little.

"Talk to me, Joe," Cletus said. "I took y'in when you had nowheres to go, gave you a home, and you kill my daughter? Don't you have nothin' to say to me?"

Joe looked utterly vacant, as if the man were no longer there. Then, slowly, one corner of his mouth curved into a smirk. "Man, Cletus. She was a damn good lay—"

BAM! BAM!

The heavy gun bucked in Cletus's hand as he fired point-blank into his brother's face. He must have been using hollow points, because the back of Joe's head literally exploded. High-impact blood spatter from the entrance and exit wounds flew in every direction. I was within five feet of Joe when the slugs hit, so I was covered from head to toe; Tracy suffered much the same as I did.

I spun, reaching for my weapon, but Cletus threw his gun, an antique 1911 .45 semi-automatic, down just as I brought mine to bear. Then he slowly sank to his knees, his face in his hands, crying softly.

I glanced at what was left of Joe Thomas. His body was slouched down in the chair, his head back, blood dripping from the gaping exit wounds.

Suicide by Cletus. Holy—

I holstered my Glock, took Tracy's cuffs from him, and...

"Cletus Thomas, I'm arresting you for the murder of Joseph Thomas...."

CHAPTER 18

"So, tell me, how does it feel, now that you have the first one under your belt?"

I thought about it, sipping on the cool glass of Krug.

Hmmm, nice. I hope he has more.

The truth was, I didn't know how I felt. I'd solved the case in record time, less than five days. But now I had that hollow, empty feeling, like I'd been wrung out. Tired? Maybe, but I didn't think so.

"It seems a bit surreal, I suppose. I feel elated on the one hand, worn out on the other." I stared into the glass, let the bubbles burst inside my nose. "How did you feel when you solved your first case?" I asked.

"It was the best feeling I ever had. Better than beating August on the golf course, better than sex... except with you, that is."

I laughed. "Nice recovery."

"So, what tipped you off?" he asked.

"Nothing I can put my finger on, but didn't... don't

you always say that if you eliminate the impossible, then what's left is the answer?"

"No, that's not what I said. I said... Well, Sherlock Holmes said... No, Arthur Conan Doyle said: 'Once you eliminate the impossible, whatever remains, no matter how improbable, must be the truth.'"

"Yes, that. Well, when I heard that Russell Hawkins had been shot, I knew... well, I knew it couldn't have been him. I had only two suspects. If you eliminate one of them, Hawkins, the other must be the perp, right? Joe Thomas."

"If it wasn't random, yes."

"Oh, hell, I never did think it was random. Someone kept the girl alive for five days. That's not the work of a random operator. You know that."

He nodded.

"But," I said, "as it almost always is, it was the science that got him. Mike Willis gets a lot of the credit. He's awesome."

"That he is. How's Hawkins doing?"

"He's doing okay, I guess. I talked to him earlier this afternoon, after we arrested Cletus... Oh man, do I feel sorry for him. First he loses his daughter in the most God-awful way, then he finds out that it was his brother that killed her, and now he's facing ten-to-life for murder."

"Nah," Harry said. "Extenuating circumstances. Once they get the facts, they'll probably charge him with second degree manslaughter: five years, maybe even less."

"I truly hope so. But to answer your question, Hawkins may never walk again, and there's talk that they may have to amputate. That's pretty hard on a man that's only in his thirties, don't you think?"

Harry blew out a breath. "I don't know, Kate. Given a choice, I think I'd go for the amputation. If he keeps his legs, he'll be in pain for the rest of his days and may never walk again. But with prosthetics... well, thanks to our boys in uniform, those have come a long way these last ten years or so."

I nodded, and held out my glass for a refill.

"So," he said, with a grin. "How are you getting along with your new partner?"

"I'm not. I had the chief transfer him. He'll be back in Narcotics tomorrow morning. Now, if you don't mind, I've had enough of all the talking."

I stood and placed my glass on the table. With a shrug of one shoulder I let the slip—all I had on—fall off my shoulders and onto the floor. "I need something a little stronger than champagne. You up for it? And I do mean *up*."

Oh, yeah. Harry was up for it.

THANK YOU FOR TAKING THE TIME TO READ JASMINE, THE FIRST IN THE SPIN-OFF SERIES OF NOVELS FEATURING LIEUTENANT KATE GAZZARA. IF YOU ENJOYED THIS STORY, YOU'LL LOVE THE NEXT BOOK.

CASSANDRA: CASE TWO. AVAILABLE IN EBOOK, PAPERBACK, & AUDIO.

BUT THERE'S MORE

If you're familiar with the Harry Starke novels, you already knew who Kate was. If not, well maybe you'd like to read them too. What follows on the next page is the first chapter of book one in the Harry Starke Novels series—there are 19 of them to date (2022). Turn the page to read a sample.

HARRY STARKE

THE HARRY STARKE NOVELS BOOK 1

By

Blair Howard

CHAPTER 1

IT WAS JUST AFTER MIDNIGHT. THE WIND WAS howling through the ironwork, blowing in off the river, and it was snowing, almost a blizzard, small flakes flying fast, horizontal. I was cold. I pulled my collar up around my ears, leaned over the parapet, and stared down into the darkness. The lights from the aquarium and the Market Street Bridge sparkled on the surface of the water.

Whitecaps on a river? I remember thinking. *What the hell am I doing here?*

A good question, and one for which I had no good answer. I'd spent the hours before midnight at the Sorbonne, a fancy name for a dump of ill repute, one of Chattanooga's sleaziest bars. I frequented it more often than I probably should, mostly to keep an eye on the lowlifes that inhabit the place. It's what I do.

Yes, I'd had a couple of drinks. Yes, really, it *was* only two, and no, I wasn't drunk. If you want to know the truth, I was bored, bored out of my brains watching the drunken idiots hitting on women they didn't know were hookers. At first it was kind of funny, then just pathetic. Finally, I'd had enough. I left the Sorbonne a little before twelve. The company had been bad, the liquor terrible, and the music... well... *How do they listen to that stuff?*

Late as it was, I wasn't ready to go home. So I figured I'd take a walk, wander the streets a little, then grab a cab and go to bed. It was a stupid thing to do. Chattanooga isn't the friendliest town at midnight in winter, but there I was on the Walnut Street Bridge, freezing my ass off, staring down into the water, and... I was a little nervous.

I wasn't worried I might get mugged. Far from it. I'm a big guy, an ex-cop, and I was carrying a concealed weapon in a shoulder rig under my left arm. But there was something in the air that night, something other than the driving snow, and I could feel it. Something I couldn't put my finger on. It made my skin crawl.

I'd walked the few yards north on Broad, turned right on Fifth, then left on Walnut, and from there to the bridge, a pedestrian-only walkway across the Tennessee River to North Shore.

I was still on the south side, on the second span, leaning on the parapet looking west along Riverfront Parkway. I must have been standing there shivering for more than thirty minutes when I saw her. Well, I heard her first. She was on Walnut, running toward me, her heels clicking on the sidewalk. I recognized her. I'd seen her earlier, in the Sorbonne.

She'd been sitting at the bar with two men, two tough-looking creeps, one tall and black with slicked back hair, the other one not so black, better dressed, smaller, and obviously the alpha. They were both wearing those shiny, quilted jackets. I'd wondered at the time what the hell she was doing there with them. She was out of their league by a mile: a classy, good-looking woman who looked as if she'd be more at home at the country club than at Benny Hinkle's sleazy dive.

She was maybe twenty-six or twenty-seven years old and wearing one of those little black dresses that cling and stick to every curve. She had red hair. Not that gaudy, fiery orange kids seem to go for these days—a muted amber that was either her own or had cost more than most people earned in a week. But it was her face that grabbed you. She might have been right out of one of those glossy fashion mags, a face that could only have come from good breeding —wow, there's an old-fashioned term—and I remember thinking, *She's probably the wife or daughter of one of the movers and shakers up on the mountain.* Add the pair of four-inch black stilettoes and the white cashmere parka that could only have come from 5th Avenue or Rodeo Drive, and I knew immediately that she was no ordinary, working-class pickup.

So what's she doing here arguing with those two? I remember thinking. I also remembered how I shook my head and stared at her legs. They seemed to go all the way up to her ears, and then some.

But I didn't dwell on her for long. I was too wrapped up in my own workaday problems to give a damn, but there was something about her that caught my interest and wouldn't let go.

Now here she was in the wind and snow, running, frightened, looking back over her shoulder as if she were being chased. Then she tripped, stumbled, almost fell. I started toward her, but as soon as she saw me, she stopped. She put her hands to her mouth, looked desperately about her, then turned, ran to the rail, and started to climb.

"No!" I shouted as I sprinted the few yards that separated us, but I was too late. She was on the rail before I could reach her.

She looked wildly around, first along Walnut and then at me... and then she jumped.

I dove the last couple of yards, my arms outstretched, and managed to grab the collar of that fancy parka with both hands. I slammed into the rail. Man, she was heavy. I hung onto the fabric, hauled on it as hard as I could, but it wasn't enough. She simply threw her arms over her head, slipped out of it, and fell. I barely heard the splash over the noise of the wind howling through the ironwork overhead. I leaned over the rail and looked down. Nothing, just the white caps on the river some eighty feet below. She wouldn't last more than a few minutes in those icy waters, supposing she'd even survived the fall.

I took out my cell and dialed 911. There was nothing else I could do. I told the operator what had happened, gave her my name and location, and sat down on one of the bench seats to wait, the parka folded over my lap. Then I lifted it up. It was heavy.

Okay, okay. I'm a nosy son of a bitch. But I'm a private detective, and the temptation was just too much. I searched the pockets. I didn't find much. There was a set of keys to a BMW in one, and a pair of white cashmere gloves and an iPhone 6 in the other. I pulled down the zipper at the front, looked at the tag and inside of the collar: Neiman Marcus. In the inside pocket I found a leather clutch, pale blue, with a snap closure at the top. It was unusual, obviously expensive, and a little larger than those handy little accessories most trendy young women like to carry. I opened it and rifled through the contents. *Geez. $2,300 in hundreds, and God knows how much in fifties and twenties.*

I put the money back, fiddled some more, found three business cards—also expensive—and a key. An ordinary key, as far as I could tell. The cards read "Tabitha Willard." Her address? Her occupation? Nada. There was nothing on it other than the name and a phone number. I searched the purse and all of her pockets again, but again found no driver's license, no ID. *Keys to a Beemer, but no license. That's strange.*

By now, I could hear sirens, so I returned everything to the purse... well, everything except one of the cards, which I slipped into my own overcoat pocket, and returned the purse to the inside pocket of the parka.

"What the hell have you done now, Starke?"

I might have known. It took only my name and a 911 call to attract the attention of the CPD in general, and Sergeant Lonnie Guest in particular. That bastard hated my guts and didn't care who knew it. He had since we were at the police academy together. He couldn't get his head around how tough it had been for him, and how easy for me. I always wondered how he'd made it through at all, much less passed the final exam.

Then I'd found out: the SOB was a cousin to the mayor. Hah, even that didn't help him much. As soon as the cousin lost the election, Lonnie lost his support. He made sergeant eight years ago, just before the mayor left office. It was His Honor's last official act, his way of getting back at the city for not supporting him. Lonnie's going nowhere in the department, has no chance of promotion. The dumbass can't pass the lieutenant's exam.

I looked up at him and smiled the smile I knew chapped his jaw.

"Not a thing, Lonnie. I just made the call. She went over the rail into the water. I managed to save her coat. Here you go." I tossed it to him.

He caught it and scowled, first at the coat, then at me.

"You're trouble, Starke. Nothin' but trouble. You may have the rest of 'em flimflammed, but not me. We shoulda locked you away years ago. Tell me what happened."

"Nah. I'll wait till someone who knows what they're doing gets here. No point in spilling it all twice."

"You'll tell me, you arrogant son of a bitch. I'm first officer on the scene."

"So you are, Lonnie, so you are. Is that soup you have on your shirt?"

He looked down.

I laughed. "Gotcha."

"Screw you, Starke, you piece of shit."

I looked at my watch, took out my phone, texted Lieutenant Gazzara, and asked her to come on down. She would not be pleased.

"Suicide, Lonnie. She ran along Walnut like the devil was after her, spotted me, and hopped over the rail. Gone, Lonnie. Into the river. Suicide."

The phone vibrated in my pants pocket. I pulled it out, unlocked it, and read the text.

"Now look, Lonnie, Kate Gazzara will be here in just a few, so why don't you go back to your cruiser where it's nice and warm, maybe take a nap, and I'll just hang out on this bench until she arrives."

"One of these days she ain't gonna be around to save your ass, Starke, an' I wanna be there when that happens."

"Yeah, well. In the meantime, you probably should make some calls, get some boats down there, and divers too. Not that they'll find anything in this mess." I looked up into the swirling snowstorm. It must have been blowing twenty miles an hour at least.

"Who the hell d'you think you are, Starke, givin' me orders? You just keep your trap shut and let us do our job, okay?" Then he did as he was told. He got on the phone and requested help from the Tennessee Wildlife river patrol and a dive team. Hah!

I grinned and settled down to wait, but not for long. Kate arrived less than five minutes later in an unmarked car, and I was right; she didn't look happy.

"This had better be good, Harry, bringing me out in this weather. I'd been home less than ten minutes when you texted. I was on my way to bed." She sat down on the bench beside me.

I turned to look at her. She always amazed me. No matter what time of day or night, Kate always looked good: almost six feet tall, slender figure—ripped, I suppose is how you would describe it—because she works out a lot. When she's at work, she keeps her long tawny hair tied back, but it was down just then, cascading around her shoulders, whipped by the wind. She has huge hazel eyes and a high forehead. She was wearing jeans tucked into high-heeled boots that came almost up to her knees, and a white turtle-neck sweater under a short, tan leather jacket. Even at one o'clock in the morning in the middle of a snowstorm, she looked stunning.

"So tell me what happened."

And I did. I told her the events of the past forty minutes, culminating with the girl taking a dive from the bridge. She didn't interrupt. She listened carefully to every word, nodding every now and then, and then she started asking questions.

"So, Harry..." She looked me in the eye. "Slumming again, huh? Why do you do it? Why do you go to places like the Sorbonne?"

"Just keeping my ear to the ground. It's in places like the Sorbonne where you learn things, not the fancy bars and restaurants."

"So... what did you find in her pockets?"

"Kate!" I tried to sound indignant, as if going through the woman's clothing was something I would never even think of doing, but she knows me better than I know myself. She tilted her head sideways and raised her eyebrows, an unspoken question.

"Okay." I sighed and shook my head. "Yes, I glanced through her stuff."

She rolled her eyes. Of course I had.

"I hung onto this." I handed her the card. "There are two more just like it in her purse, wallet, whatever the hell it is. There's also a wad of cash, and a fob for a late-model BMW, the keyless type. No driver's license, though. Strange, huh?"

She nodded, fingered the card, turned it over, and looked at the back. "Hey! Sergeant Guest." She had to shout to be heard over the wind. "Bring that coat over here, will you please?"

Please? I'd have told the creep to get his fat ass over here, and quick, but I guess she's more lady than she is cop... Nope, that isn't true. The lady's a lady, but she's all cop.

We both watched as the big sergeant leaned inside his cruiser and retrieved the parka.

He backed out of the car, then sauntered over. The look on his face was a treat to behold too, when he dropped the coat on her lap. He looked like he'd just bitten into a lemon.

"Might be a good idea to search this light-fingered piece of garbage while you're at it, LT," he said with a smirk. "There's a whole lot o' cash in the wallet. Some of it might o' stuck to Starke here." He nodded down at me.

I grinned back up at him.

"That's enough of that talk, Sergeant. How long before Wildlife and the divers get here?"

"They're on their way. Shouldn't be too much longer. I'll go wait in the cruiser, if it's okay with you."

"Yeah, go on. I'll call if I need you." She waited until he was back inside his car before she handed me the card. "I didn't give you that. If anyone asks, you stole it, right?"

I nodded. "Kate, the girl was frightened out of her mind. She seemed fine when I saw her earlier in the bar with two nasty-looking creeps. What the hell could have scared her like that? And what was she doing with those two? I've seen them around, but I don't know who they are. She was a lovely kid, Kate. I want to know what happened."

She didn't answer. She got to her feet, unfolded the parka, and let out a low whistle. "Whoa, cashmere, Neiman Marcus.

This little number must have set her back at least four grand, maybe more. What I wouldn't give for one of these." She tucked the coat under her arm and opened the clutch.

"How much money is in here, Harry?" She rifled through the wad of bills.

"I'm not sure."

"Twenty-three hundreds, along with nine fifties and eight twenties: $2,910 in all. That's a lot of cash to be carrying around loose, especially into a place like the Sorbonne. What could she have been thinking?"

I nodded, but I didn't say anything. The divers were arriving on Riverfront Parkway, and there were blue lights flashing on the river; Tennessee Wildlife was there, too.

"Okay, Harry. You'd better take off and go home. Oh, and, Harry, I know you're going to be looking into this; you can't help yourself. This time, though, that's probably a good thing, because we can't. It's a suicide, plain and simple; you said so yourself. We'll try to identify her, contact her next of kin, and... well, you know how it goes. When we do, I'll call you, but you're right; from what you saw in the bar, there may be something more going on. If so, we need to know about it. That's on you, Harry. I'll help, if I can, but stay out of trouble, and keep that damn gun in its holster. One more incident like the last one, and I won't be able to save you. You got that?"

She was talking about something I'd done a couple of months ago. I had to pull my weapon on a suspect. Turned out the guy was innocent. He didn't press charges, but the police weren't too happy about it. It wasn't the first time they didn't like something I did, though, and it surely wouldn't be the last.

"Got it. I'll start first thing in the morning." I looked at my watch. "Damn, it already *is* morning."

"Harry, if you find anything, anything at all, call me, please. Otherwise, we'll stay in touch by text, right?"

I agreed. She folded the Neiman Marcus and walked slowly, head down, back to her car. As she passed Guest's patrol unit, she stopped, leaned in the window, and said something I didn't hear. Two minutes later, she hit the starter, did a three-point turn, sped off along Walnut, then turned left on East 4th, heading toward the hospital, going home, I supposed.

I didn't wait until morning. I walked off the bridge onto Walnut, then turned right and found a bench outside the aquarium. I took the card out of my pocket and punched the number into my phone.

"Yeah?" A male voice.

"Tabitha Willard, please?"

Click.

Son of a bitch. He hung up. I tried again, but there was no answer.

Okay, so it would have to wait until the city was awake. Bed seemed like a good idea.

I checked my watch. 1:15. I called a cab, then hunkered down in a doorway, out of the wind, and waited.

It was no more than a fifteen-minute ride to my place at that time in the morning. I paid the cabbie, slipped him an extra ten and wished him goodnight, what was left of it.

I threw my coat down on a chair in the kitchen, poured myself a stiff measure of Laphroaig Quarter Cask scotch and flung myself down on the sofa in front of the picture window. The wind and snow had slacked off almost to nothing, just a light breeze and a few flurries. A light mist covered the surface of the river, a soft gray blanket that swirled and undulated, turning the mighty Tennessee into a living thing. The view from my window was, as always, spectacular.

I lay there, staring out over the water, savoring the ten-year-old malt. My brain was in overdrive. The events of the past few hours came flooding back. Time after time, I saw the horrified look on the girl's face when she spotted me. I kept remembering the way she dropped, slowly turning end over end, splashing into the murky water far below. Was there anything else I could have done to save her? I was sure the question would haunt me for the rest of my days... and nights. There'd be no sleep for me that night.

Geez, what a way to go.

CHAPTER 2

I WOKE TO A BRIGHT, SUNNY MORNING... LATE, BUT still morning, the sound of my cell phone jangling in my ear. *Geez, already? I have to change that damned ring tone.*

"Starke."

"Harry, it's Kate. Where are you?"

"Still home. Why? What's up?"

"Still home? Do you know what time it is?"

"Er... no. You woke me up. I don't even know what day it is."

"Harry, it's Tuesday. It's almost eleven."

"Eleven? Damn. I overslept."

"We need to meet. I have some news."

I looked at my watch. "My office. Give me an hour. Noon? I'll buy you lunch."

"Okay, see you then."

Damn! Eleven o'clock already. I'm going to have to quit with the booze... Nah.

I took one last look out over the river and hopped out of bed. In the kitchen, I hit the go button on the coffee maker for a large cup of coffee, then went back to my bedroom, stripped, and took a long cold shower.

Ten minutes later I was dressed and on my way downtown.

I run a private investigation agency in Chattanooga, with a small suite of offices just a couple of blocks from the Flatiron Building on Georgia Avenue. It's close to the courts and law offices—a great location for what I do. I work for a whole range of clients, from lawyers to corporate entities to members of the general public.

I employ a staff of nine, including five investigators, two secretaries, an intern, and my personal assistant, Jacque Hale.

I know just about everyone who matters, not only in Chattanooga, but also in Atlanta, Birmingham, and Nashville, not the least of whom is my old man. It's not what you know, but who you know, right?

My father, August Starke, is a lawyer, a very good one. He specializes in tort, which is a classy word for personal injury. You've probably seen him on TV. His ads run on most local stations almost every day. He made sure that I got the best education money could buy. I graduated McCallie in '91—and so did most of the movers and shakers in this city of ours; not all in '91 of course—and I have a master's degree in forensic psychology from Fairleigh Dickinson.

My agency does a lot of work for my father. His latest claim to fame was his successful class action lawsuit against one of the big drug companies. He brought in millions in compensation for local victims of the birth control fiasco. Now he has his teeth into another case: some of the new high-tech blood thinners seem to be causing more problems than cures. We're doing some work for him on that one, too.

It was right at noon when I walked into my office. I'm not usually that late. I make it a habit to be at my desk no later than seven thirty. The rest of the crew is expected in no later than eight, unless they're on assignment.

Kate was already there when I arrived, seated in one of those leather chesterfield chairs that seem to be the obligatory norm in most professional offices. She was wearing jeans, a black sweater, and the same tan leather jacket she'd worn the night before. Her hair was pulled back and tied in a ponytail. She, and everyone else, looked up when I walked in. They all grinned.

"Okay, so I'm late, dammit."

I rolled my eyes, beckoned for Kate to follow me, and went into my inner sanctum. I waited until she'd seated herself, then I poked my head out the door, caught Mike's attention, pointed at the coffee pot, and raised two fingers.

Now, I have to tell you, there's really only one place where I'm truly happy, other than my condo, and that's my office. It's as comfortable as I could possibly make it. It has all the trimmings: the big desk, leather chairs, computer, and all, but I also spent a lot of money on the decor. The walls are paneled with dark walnut; there are two floor-to-ceiling bookshelves; the ceiling itself is painted a soft magnolia color; the carpet is pure wool—dark red. The window is covered with ivory sheers accented with heavy drapes that match the carpet. The artwork, a half-dozen pieces, is original—local scenes by local artists—not worth a fortune, but costly enough. There's also a small drinks cabinet where I keep my special goodies. The room had been designed by a master. Her intention was to instill in my clients a sense of opulence and success, and I think she succeeded. Kate laughingly calls it my man cave.

I didn't take the seat behind my desk. Instead, I sat in the one next to Kate. Mike brought the coffee. Life was good.

Kate looked around the room. "Do you ever miss being a cop, Harry?"

"Nope. What about you? You need to get out of that rat race, too. Come work for me. You'll make more money."

"Hah, not a chance. And what the hell would you do without me on the inside if I did?"

"Good question. I'd work it out. Don't I always? So tell me: what about the girl?"

"They found her an hour after we left. I saw her this morning. What a damn shame."

I nodded, said nothing, and waited for her to continue.

"The name on the business card was correct. She is —*was*—Tabitha Willard. The phone number is disconnected."

"It wasn't at one o'clock this morning. I called it. A male answered. He hung up when I asked for her. Were you able to trace it?"

"Nope. It was probably a burner."

"That doesn't mean it can't be traced. They have to be activated, right?"

She nodded.

"That will tell us where it was purchased. If it came from one of the big stores, they usually have security cameras, and that means photos. Photos can be identified. I'll have Tim look into it."

She nodded again and sipped her coffee.

"How did you identify her?"

"Her prints are on file. Shoplifting. A year ago."

"So who is she? Where's she from? Geez, Kate. Don't make me drag it out of you."

"She's the daughter of Justin Willard. Ring any bells?"

"Not that I can think of. Who is he?"

"One of our best-loved plastic surgeons. If you need to get rid of the wrinkles? He's the man. Need new tits? He's the man. Need a new face? Well, you get the idea. He's been around a long time. Impeccable reputation. Rich as Croesus."

"That rich, huh? Okay. So, have you informed the family?"

"Oh yeah. I went up there myself, just before I came here. I also went and had a word with her sister Jessica and Charlotte Maxwell, Tabitha's best friend. And, by the way, I told the good doctor to expect you."

"Up there? On Lookout, right?"

"Yep! It's on Cheatham Avenue. Nice place. Must be worth a couple of mil."

"So?"

"Hell, Harry, they hadn't even missed her. She lived in an apartment over the garage. Why would anyone want a six-car garage? It must have cost almost as much to build as the home. Harry, the man drives a Rolls Royce; he owns a damn jet, for God's sake."

"Hah, so does my father—own a jet, not a Rolls—and

there are more than a few around here who own one of those, too. I think I'd like to have me one someday."

She looked at me; her expression was priceless.

"Joking, Kate. Joking. What did he say when you told him I was coming to see him?"

"He said for you to call first to make sure he was home. If not, he said you can go by his office. Other than that, he didn't seem bothered about you visiting. But maybe it didn't register. He *was* kind of upset." She leaned over the desk, grabbed a pen, and scribbled a number on the blotter. "That's his home number. He wouldn't give me his cell. His office number is in the book."

I nodded. "Okay, so tell me about Tabitha."

"There's not much to tell. They found her less than a hundred yards from the bridge. Her neck was broken, probably from the fall. She was wearing a black dress, no shoes—you said she was wearing some when she went over so we're assuming they came off in the water—a Rolex watch, a couple of gold bracelets, both eighteen karat, and..." She looked at me and then continued: "no underwear."

I grinned at her. Nah, I smirked. "None?"

She rolled her eyes. "No, pervert, none at all. No bra, no panties, nothing."

"She may have lost the panties when she hit the water." I grinned at her. "I've lost my trunks more than once, making a splash."

"True. That could be it. She was also wearing this."

She handed me a thin gold chain with a pendant attached. The pendant was in the form of two serpents entwined, each swallowing the other's tail. It was quite small, not much bigger than a quarter. It was unique. I'd never seen anything like it before.

"What is it, Kate?"

"Search me. It's unusual, eighteen-karat gold, the chain, too, and expensive, like everything else about her. Her father said he hadn't seen it before, so did her sister and her friend, which I thought was strange... Maybe you should check it out. Anyway, that's about all I've got. Now you know more than I do. Let's go get some lunch. Your treat."

"Sure, as always."

"Oh come *on*, Harry. You can afford it."

"That I can, but it would be nice if you offered, just once."

"Okay then. My treat. The Deli?"

I nodded. We both rose to our feet.

"Kate?"

"Yeah?"

"Can I borrow the pendant? Just for a day or two?"

She shook her head. "I'd rather not. It's valuable, and I'd be in serious trouble if you lost it."

I tilted my head sideways. "Okay, let me get a picture of it then." She put it down on my desk, and I snapped a photo with my iPhone.

"That ought to do it. Let's go." I handed her the pendant, and we left the office.

"One more thing, Harry." She reached into her jacket pocket, bringing out the key she'd taken from the girl's pocket. "Here. Take it. I have no idea what it's for. Neither did the old man or her sister, or her friend. Maybe it means something. Maybe it doesn't."

I nodded, slipped the key into the pocket of my jacket,

and then followed her out onto the street. It's always nice to follow Kate. She has some great assets.

The Flatiron Deli is housed in the building that bears the same name, just a couple of blocks away from my office, very handy, and the food is good, too. They make the best BLT in town. I ordered one of those with a cup of coffee. Kate had a Muffaletta, a Coke, and a loaded baked potato to go with it.

How does she eat all those calories and keep the weight off?

We sat opposite each other in a booth. We ate quietly for a while, then we both spoke at once.

I smiled at her. "Ladies first."

"I was about to tell you that we found her car. It was parked in the multi-story near the aquarium. It was clean, Harry, and by clean I mean it had been wiped; it was spotless."

"Hmmm."

She nodded. "What about those two you saw her with in the bar? You said you've seen them before?"

I nodded and said, "I've seen them a couple of times. They were a weird pair. For some reason, they reminded me of Stimpy and Ren." She smiled at that, and I continued, "One was a tall, well-built guy, black, with slicked back hair, arrogant. The smaller guy was clean-shaven, lighter skinned, assertive. I got the feeling that he was running the show. I couldn't hear what they were talking about, but I could tell they were arguing. She was holding her own, though."

I looked at my watch. It was almost two o'clock.

"Kate, I think I'll head down that way, to the Sorbonne, see if I can get anything out of Benny Hinkle. He was running the bar last night. You done?"

She got up from the booth. "Good idea. Call me later. Let me know if you find anything. When do you expect to go see Willard?"

"I was thinking I'd head up that way early this evening. You want to go?"

"Can't. Hot date. Don't forget to call him first." She leaned over, pecked me on the cheek, then walked quickly out of the Deli. You guessed it. She'd stiffed me for the tab, and the tip. I had to grin. She was a rare one. And then it hit me.

Hot date? What was that about? Kate never dates. Well, just me, I think.

I returned to my office, gave Tim the phone number on Tabitha Willard's card, and asked him to see if he could track it down. I made a couple of calls, then headed out again.

CONTINUE READING BOOK 1 OF THE HARRY STARKE NOVELS.

Available in eBook, Paperback, Hardcover, & Audio.

Genesis - "As always with Blair Howard's books, there are lots of dead ends and twists and turns . . . Great read!" *Alice - Amazon Reviewer*

Would you like to get a free copy of the first book in my best-selling Harry Starke Genesis series?
Visit www.blairhowardbooks.com

THANK YOU

Once again, I'd like to thank you for reading Jasmine. If you liked it, perhaps you would consider posting a short review on Amazon (just a sentence will do). Word of mouth is an author's best friend and much appreciated.

To those many of my readers who have already posted reviews to this and my other novels, thank you for your past and continued support.

VISIT MY WEBSITE AT
WWW.BLAIRHOWARDBOOKS.COM.

From Blair Howard

The Harry Starke Genesis Series

The Harry Starke Series

The Lt. Kate Gazzara Murder Files

The Peacemaker Series

The O'Sullivan Chronicles: Civil War Series

From Blair C. Howard

The Science Fiction Sovereign Star Series

ABOUT THE AUTHOR

Blair Howard is a retired journalist turned novelist. He's the author of more than 40 novels including the international best-selling Harry Starke series of crime stories, the Lt. Kate Gazzara series, and the Harry Starke Genesis series. He's also the author of the Peacemaker series of international thrillers and five Civil War/Western novels.

If you enjoy reading Science Fiction thrillers, Mr. Howard has made his debut into the genre with, The Sovereign Stars Series under the name, Blair C. Howard.

Visit www.blairhowardbooks.com.

You can also find Blair Howard on Social Media

Made in the USA
Las Vegas, NV
23 August 2023